The Jinxed Journalist

The Borderline Chronicles, Volume 3

Fiona West

Published by Tempest and Kite, 2019.

This is a work of fiction. Similarities to real people, places, or events are entirely coincidental.

THE JINXED JOURNALIST

First edition. October 11, 2019.

CHAPTER ONE

ONCE UPON A TIME—A long time ago, but not so long that people don't remember—a beautiful princess lived in a kingdom high in the mountains. Her name was Giselle, and as happy and joyful as her life was, she longed for a handsome prince. Not to help her rule; she'd been groomed from the time she was young for that role. Not to keep her warm at night; she had quilts and coverlets enough. But someone to talk to, to laugh with. Giselle wanted a friend.

And so, when Prince Ralstand rode into the kingdom to ask for her hand in marriage, Giselle was delighted.

Unfortunately, Ralstand was not willing to play second fiddle to anyone, certainly not a princess from a backwater territory such as this. Unable to attract a woman who was willing to let him rule, he plotted another path to his desires. He was well versed in magic, and it had made him proud, arrogant. He had come for a kingdom, and he was going to get it by any means possible. His hidden agenda would not be discovered until it was all too late. On the night of their wedding, Ralstand pulled Giselle out onto the balcony alone, hidden among the ivy-laden pillars, and, taking her face in his hands, he kissed her. But this was no ordinary kiss . . . Giselle went to bed that night and never woke again. Having married her already, Ralstand claimed her kingdom and ruled in her stead, the curse holding his wife in place, stuck between life and death in eternal, dreamless sleep.

Ralstand's Kiss is now an illegal magical maneuver in every country on the continent and across the Sparkling Sea.

BROOKE WALKED DOWN the streets of East Cheekton to her favorite café.

"Hi, Jerry," she said to the man sitting in old clothes by the front door. "How was your night?"

He shrugged, mumbling to himself.

She knelt to see him better. "Hungry?"

His eyes lit up, and she smiled as she pulled a soft granola bar out of her purse. He didn't thank her as he ripped into the packaging . . . He was usually a bit more cogent than this, and his current state worried Brooke. But her mind was elsewhere as she went inside, ordered her tea, and found a table where she could see the door. She waited until her mug of peppermint tea had gone cold in front of her. She doodled trees in the margins of her yellow legal pad, bouncing her knee, her phone on the table beside her, faceup, ready to record. Her source should've been here by now. Maybe she should've picked her up at the airfield; blimps' arrival times were notoriously unpredictable. *Or maybe she changed her mind. Maybe I'm in deep sugar.* She'd taken to curbing her use of profanities, even in her head, or they came out in front of her five-year-old. She smiled as a reflex when her sandy-haired boy came to mind. Pride and joy didn't come close, didn't even nick the surface of how she felt about her kid.

The bell on the café door tinkled as the door opened, and she looked up. *Not my contact.* She sighed, pulling out her notes to review them. Their phone conversation had been productive, but she wanted more of the story. Her first week as a reporter for *Orangiers Today*, and she was going to blow the lid right off a scandal so big no one else in the office had wanted to touch it. She was going to make a name for herself and right an injustice at the same time . . . It almost felt too good to be true. *Maybe it is. Maybe I should just leave now, before she gets here . .* .

The bell tinkled again, and this time, it was her. The curvy red-haired white woman was scanning the room, and Brooke waved. She looked older than she'd inferred from their initial conversation, and it took Brooke a minute to recalibrate her thoughts before she opened her mouth. The man trailing her was her husband, Brooke presumed. Black hair, well dressed, white skin. She rose from her seat and held out a hand to Greta first.

"Mrs. Burnham. I'm Brooke Everleigh." She shook her hand firmly and took a seat.

"This is my husband, Ralph."

"Nice to meet you," Brooke said, turning her attention to him briefly. "I'm glad you brought someone with you to support you. I'm sure it won't be easy reliving these memories. But I want you to know that I'm going to do everything possible to bring your story to light, to help hold the perpetrator accountable for the terrible crime he committed against you."

Greta's gaze was on the table, and her shoulders were hunched as she twisted her fingers in her lap. All the confidence she'd had when she entered the café was now gone. Her husband put a hand on her back.

"She finds it quite difficult to talk about, you know?" He said, rubbing his wife's shoulders.

"I'm sure. Please, take your time. Can I get you a drink?" She'd get another for herself, but her budget was tight enough as it was.

"No." She shook her head. "I just want to get this over with."

Brooke nodded, clicking the point out of her pen; she still preferred pen and paper to technology. No one was going to hack her notes—her handwriting was indecipherable. "Let's get started, then." She started the voice recording app on her phone. "You mentioned on the phone that the man who gave you Ralstand's Kiss was a high-profile political figure, but you didn't mention whom. Are you ready to tell me now?"

Greta's unsteady green gaze met Brooke's. "Yes, Ms. Everleigh. The man who kissed me is none other than Edward, king of Orangiers."

Brooke dropped her pen in surprise, then scrambled to retrieve it. "When did this happen?"

"I was involved with the war effort, and I had some contact with His Majesty as a member of the Attaamish delegation assigned to help with logistics. We were meeting to discuss the possibility of the Attaamish Special Forces going to Trella. The next thing I knew, my husband was shaking me awake. I had been missing for four days."

"I take it your husband is magically inclined?"

He nodded. "I'm registered in Attaamy. I was able to break the curse because of my close connection with Greta. I've been building a secondary relationship with the magic on her behalf for years." He gazed at her lovingly. "You can never be too careful."

Brooke nodded, still scribbling everything down. "I hate to ask this, because your word should be enough, but do you have any more proof that Edward was involved?"

Greta reached into her purse, then placed a ring on the table. "I was found holding this."

Brooke picked it up. It was clearly not a normal ring; it was too finely made, the delicate metalwork scrolling that held the ruby too perfect. It was masculine-looking; around the base, filigree mimicked waves, and in the setting a ship appeared to be carrying the stone, common symbols of the royal family in Orangiers.

"I looked it up on the internet. It's his. He was seen wearing it at his sister's engagement party a few months ago," Greta's husband put in, taking the ring back from Brooke. "Perhaps there was a struggle when he tried to kiss her? We don't know how it happened, but you can talk to Colonel Gasper—he was there when she was found."

"Edward's number two on the battlefield? That's the same man, right?"

"That's right," Ralph said. "Greta started saying things afterward, little flashes started coming back to her." He rubbed her back again as he gazed at her sadly. "Then a few days ago, she remembered everything."

CHAPTER TWO

I CAN'T WAIT TO BLINDSIDE this guy. Brooke sat in the padded blue chairs of the palace briefing room, staring at the man behind the podium. *Early twenties, dark-blonde hair neatly styled, dazzling smile, chest like a brick wall, immaculate blue uniform.* Her knee bounced incessantly. This guy, this somewhat intimidating military guy, was what stood between her and breaking the story that she'd uncovered. "Flirt like your life depends on it," her predecessor had advised. "He's a pushover for a low-cut top, a short skirt and a pair of heels." Given that Willow had done pretty well in the ten years she'd been covering the palace, Brooke knew she was probably right. Unfortunately, that wasn't her style.

She gathered her leather messenger bag to march up to the front, when she felt a hand on her shoulder.

"Don't, don't, don't. Not yet." The gangly strawberry-blond man who unceremoniously clambered over the back of the seat next to her drew grunts of annoyance from those around them. "Just sit down, love."

"Judson, where've you been? I've been here twenty minutes."

"There was someone slow on the stairs. Besides, they never start on time." He paused, rearranging his clothes. "Well, they never did before *he* got put in charge," he said, flicking his gaze toward Captain Saint. "Military men." Judd was about as far from a military man as you could get, and she loved him for it. He was always wearing corduroy in some fashion and looked

6

constantly askew, hair mussed under various beanies, press pass about to come off his coat. They'd been best friends since he hit on her in a bar six years ago and they stayed up all night talking about journalism and politics and history. They never did make it back to anyone's apartment, exchanging phone numbers instead, promising to get coffee. The only chemistry between them was of the incombustible friendship variety. But they'd never worked together until now; she was glad to see that it didn't seem to be changing their relationship.

"How'd you know I was going to go up there?"

"You had an aura of determination about you. Same one you get when Olly pulls out a deck of cards."

She was viciously competitive when it came to things that didn't matter, even when playing against her own son.

"I want to introduce myself; otherwise, he'll never call on me."

He looked her up and down. "Didn't Willow tell you what to wear?"

She tapped her foot impatiently. "She gave me some advice. I'll do this my own way."

Judson Boote grinned at her. "This should be entertaining. Fine, go up there, put your hand out."

She stood up. "Fine, I will. You coming?"

"Oh no, he knows who I am. The bloke from the pathetic online news outlet he keeps ignoring. I'll save our seats."

"Fine."

"Fine. Go."

"I am going." Brooke took a deep breath and edged her way down the row. *Get up there, get up there quick before he . . .*

"I'd like to get started," Captain Saint said into the micro-phone.

Duck feathers, she swore inwardly. He looked up at her as her steps slowed, and she knew at once that Willow had been right when a slow smile spread across his face. Brooke wasn't stupid; even dressed in her knee-length denim skirt, high-heeled ankle boots and bohemian blouse, she was fairly good-looking. She'd heard stories about him—his reputation as a pickup artist preceded him—and she knew his type. But it was better to let him think she was friendly . . . for now. He noticed her, and the look on his face said, "I'm going to bite the buttons off your shirt without asking first." She flipped her honey-blonde hair over her shoulder and gave him a coy wave as she went back to her seat, confirming that he was still follow-ing her with his eyes. *That's right. You see me now, don't you?*

His briefing was boring; the standard things about the king's scheduled meetings and conferences during the week, when dignitaries would arrive, who they would have dinner with, what they would discuss with His Majesty, blah blah blah.

When he opened the floor for questions, she launched her hand into the air along with about twenty-five men. His eyes lingered on her before calling on a more senior member of the audience.

"Drake Fringerly, *Barrowdon Bugle.* Will the grand duchess be attending meetings set to take place between His Majesty and Prince Regent Kurt Porchenzii of Brevspor?"

"The grand duchess no longer consults on political matters for Brevspor. She will certainly engage in the social functions that take place during his visit, but she will not be privy to policy talks and discussions between the leaders of the two nations."

"Thank you, Captain."

Brooke raised her hand again, trying to look more casual this time, and considered popping loose another button on her blouse. *Desperate times.* He looked at her again, and she could tell he was debating.

"Yes, Ms. . . ."

"Everleigh. Brooke Everleigh, *Orangiers Today*. Would His Majesty like to respond to accusations by Mrs. Greta Burnham, an Attaamish civilian, that he used Ralstand's Kiss against her during the Brothers' War on the twenty-first of Fourth Month last year?"

Every eye was on her. It felt amazing. She held the captain's unreadable gaze confidently, then held out her phone to record his response.

He cleared his throat, but his face remained impassive. "The palace has no comment at this time. Next."

Shouts for attention deafened her as the formerly apathetic group of men came to life at the first sign of a juicy story.

"Is His Majesty denying contact with Mrs. Burnham?"

"Does he have an alibi for the time in question?"

"What was he trying to hide?"

"When did the king discover his magical ability? Is he registered as a user?"

Captain Saint held up his hands for silence, and the group quieted to murmurs.

"The king is not registered as a non-tech magic user, since he is not magically inclined. As I said, the palace has no comment on this 'story' at this time . . ."

Oh, he did not just air quote the word story *like I'm some rookie reporter who doesn't know what she's doing,* she seethed inwardly. But he had.

The captain answered a few more questions about the king's upcoming travels and thoughts on new environmental legislation, then dismissed the group.

"You." His steel gaze was on her as he pointed to the space next to the podium.

"Oooh," said Judson under his breath. "Do you think he knows who you are now?"

Brooke grinned as she slung her bag over her shoulder and meandered to the front of the room with as much lack of concern as she could muster. She'd always had a good poker face, but being a mother had taken her bluffing to a new level. Nobody could see through her like Olly.

The captain's eyes were a hard blue that told her he was not pleased. "Good morning, Ms. . . . Everleigh, was it?"

"Yes, good morning, Captain. Did you wish to speak with me?"

"Yes, as a matter of fact. Perhaps your predecessor didn't inform you, but when there's information of a sensitive nature, you can bring those questions to me privately, rather than trying to start a stampede in the briefing room."

She crossed her arms. "Sounds to me like you just don't want some questions asked."

"No, what I want is decorum and order in my briefing room. Not mudslinging."

"Mudslinging?" Brooke straightened her spine. "So listening to victims and believing their stories is now mudslinging? Can I quote you on that?"

"No, you may not," he said, dropping his voice to a lower register. "I'm just trying to help you learn how things are here, seeing as you're new."

"Well, thanks anyway, Captain, but I'm pursuing this story out in the open, not whispering questions into your ear. Though I hear you like that if the blouse is cut low enough. And by the way, I'm not interested in that kind of attention from you." She leaned into the podium. "That'll never happen."

Saint blinked blankly at her, then smiled. "Good luck to you, Ms. Everleigh. My guess is that I've wasted my time even learning your name." He strode from the platform before Brooke could process his insult in time to form a retort.

CHAPTER THREE

CAPTAIN SAINT WAS ON his phone dialing the king's secretary before the briefing room door had swung shut behind him.

"I need to talk to him."

"He's in a meeting with—"

"Whoever he's with, this is more important." *This is a crisis.*

"Okay. Yes. I'll try to signal him," said Ms. Scrope.

Saint sighed. "No, just—I'll come to him. Where are you?"

"Bancroft Hall."

Saint hung up without saying goodbye and strode through the halls of Bluffton, ignoring everyone he passed. He wasn't in the mood to be polite; that new reporter, clearly spoiling for a fight, had drained every drop of civility out of him. He'd noticed her right away; it would be hard not to. It wasn't just her looks . . . It was the way she carried herself. Shoulders back, a smile a whisper away from a smirk, unfidgety. But apparently, having the female equivalent of swagger also equated to an ego the size of Mount Copperfield.

Captain Saint stopped outside the hall. Dean and Waldo, the king's security detail, gave him a nod as he fell in next to them. He pulled out his phone and answered emails: a request for a private tour of the residence by a Forgelands TV station (no); a request for an interview with the grand duchess about her human trafficking work (he'd ask her); a request for Dowager Queen Lily to attend a tea to benefit homeless dogs (forwarded to her secretary). The doors opened and Edward came out first. He looked tired. He was usually perfectly put together, but today, he was missing his tie and his white shirtsleeves were rolled to his elbows, revealing his inky black skin.

"We're not scheduled to meet. Is this a social moment?"

Saint grimaced. "No. My office or yours?"

"Mine. I have another meeting in twenty. You'll have to fill me in while I eat."

"Fine."

The two men walked in silence. Being friends with a king for many years had its advantages, though he liked to believe he could've gotten this position regardless. Still, it didn't hurt to work your connections. Saint made himself wait to start filling in the details; despite his flawless outward physical appearance and pressed uniform, self-control wasn't one of his strengths. Edward, he knew, came by it naturally; he'd always been a temperate person, whereas Saint was basically holding it together until he was off duty. He'd need to let loose soon.

Saint closed the polished oak door to Edward's office behind him. "Do you recall a woman named Greta Burnham?"

"Burnham?" He shook his head as he sat down at his desk, picking up his knife and fork to cut into his steak. "Wait, yes—I believe she worked for the Attaamish delegation. Red hair?"

"Don't know her hair color, but she's claiming you gave her Ralstand's Kiss."

Edward stiffened, gripping his utensils harder. "I beg your pardon?"

"A new reporter asked me today if you'd used magic against her, Greta Burnham, during the Brothers' War. On the twenty-first of Fourth Month, no less, when you weren't even at the front."

"I wasn't, I didn't. I would never."

Saint scowled. "I know that."

Edward leaned forward, and, paired with the anger he'd expected, Saint read the vulnerability in his eyes. "I would *never*. I need you to know that. I wouldn't lie to you. I haven't any skill with magic."

Edward. So tenderhearted, he thought with mild amusement.

"Settle down, mate. I know that. I just had to ask. I had to bring this to you, to see how you wanted me to handle it. I wasn't sure if you wanted it to be common knowledge that you'd left the front in the middle of the war to escort Abbie across the Unveiled."

His friend sat back hard in his chair, his lunch forgotten, and a deep sigh burst from his chest. "I'll have to consider that." He glanced up at Saint. "Can we trust this reporter? If we disclose that I wasn't at the front, do you think she'll keep that to herself?"

Saint resisted the impulse to run his fingers through his hair. "I doubt it. She seems hungry for a story, any story. Wants to prove herself. Jersey on wheels." *Or rather, Jersey on high heels. High-heeled boots . . . and the shapely legs in those boots.*

"How would you like to proceed?"

"I can 'no comment' Ms. Everleigh for a time, but I'm not sure if that'll work. The other reporters have heard the names involved now, and they're going to go after the story themselves."

"Stick with 'no comment' for now. It's rubbish. Maybe it'll go away on its own."

"Well, that's the thing," said Saint, rubbing the back of his neck. "I do remember a story that circulated about a female delegate who'd disappeared. At the time, we all just assumed she'd had too much to drink or gone home. Gasper would know."

"Check with him, please. Even if I wasn't involved, someone was."

"Someone's got to talk to Abbie, too."

The king swore softly. "I'll do it myself."

"It has to be done today. Don't put it off."

"On second thought, perhaps you could come with me. It's your area of expertise, and . . ."

Saint grimaced. "I wouldn't want to go alone, either."

Edward sighed, his head dropping to touch his chin to his chest. "Let me eat a little, then we'll go." A staff member quietly brought Saint a plate and slipped out, and the two men chatted about less distressing things while they consumed their lunch.

"Let's get this over with," said Edward, standing.

"Right." Saint went out as Ms. Scrope came in, her arms full of reading material. "Alice," he greeted her.

"Saint." They'd shared a night together a while back, but he was determined not to let it affect his professionalism at work. From the sparkle in her eye, though, it looked like she might be interested in another round. *If I was ever tempted . . . too bad I seldom go back for seconds.*

He pulled out his phone as he stalked down the long hallway toward the residence.

Saint: Got a minute to talk? Palace business.

Abbie: SNORE. Fine.

Saint: On our way.

Abbie: Both of you? Must be serious.

Saint sighed. He liked Abbie, but she was just about the worst royal in the world. He would never put her behind a podium if he could help it. Next to it was okay; she was a pretty girl—lily-white skin, auburn curls, curvy. But he couldn't let her in range of the microphone. That was just asking for trouble. He knocked at the residence and she called out to him.

"This better be good. You're interrupting my studying."

He grinned as he closed the door behind them. "How are your classes going?"

"Good. But all those whippersnappers make me feel old; I've got to stay on my toes with the material so they don't realize how senile I am compared to them." Abbie also had lupus, which affected her memory, Saint knew. But he wouldn't mention that if she didn't bring it up. "What do you need?"

Edward sat next to her and held her hand. "We need to make you aware of an accusation that's come out."

"Oh?" She closed the thick organic chemistry book and gave him her attention.

Saint nodded. "A new reporter is accusing Edward of using magic against a woman at the front during the Brothers' War."

She frowned. "Using it against her how?"

"Ralstand's Kiss."

Abbie's gaze hardened. "That's ridiculous. He's got no magical ability; if the remote control stops working, he makes Tezza fix it." Everyone in Veiled countries relied on magic to power their communications and electronics, and the royal family was no different. But affecting someone the way Greta Burnham was, so thoroughly and for so long, would take a powerful user with more than average ability. If that was Edward, he'd hidden it extremely well.

"It is," he agreed. Saint tried to relax his shoulders; they were starting to burn. He hadn't realized how worried he'd been that she'd be upset by the situation.

"So we're not providing commentary," continued Edward, "especially considering I wasn't even in Attaamy at the time of the supposed incident."

She looked at the ceiling as realization dawned. "Right. You were with me. But we don't want anyone to know you left the front. This is going to be tricky."

"Hence my presence here to warn you about it," said Edward.

"Well, I appreciate that."

"Remember, don't talk to the press about it, Abbie," said Saint. "I'm serious. I know you have a tendency to . . ."

"Go off?" she asked, daring him to argue with her.

He nodded, backing toward the door. "Yes, to go off. But you can't on this one. Any reaction from our part will look defensive. We've got to play this one cool. All right?"

She nodded. "All right. I get it."

Saint held the door open as Edward kissed her and moved to exit, his phone already buzzing with more problems, and Abbie resumed her studying.

"We still on for hiking on Saturday?" Saint asked.

Abbie snorted. "Right."

"What's that mean, love?"

"It means you go out Friday night, meet some girl, wake up Woz knows where, and you always blow me off. That's what."

He crossed his arms. "I do not."

"You do. You think with your pants. It sucks. You suck."

She was joking, but that stung a little. "Maybe this time I won't."

"Everyone who believes that, raise your hand . . ." She kept her hands folded pointedly in her lap, and he laughed.

"See you Saturday, Grand Duchess."

"See you next week, Francis." It was their inside joke; she hated her title, so she punished him by using his first name whenever he used it.

Yeah, never in front of a microphone.

CHAPTER FOUR

IT WASN'T FAIR, BROOKE knew, to resent Olly's very short legs when she was in a hurry, but she did anyway. Dragging him by his hand up to the palace gates, she hissed at him to *come on, kiddo.* He should've been at school . . . Maybe she could get through the morning without anyone asking too many questions about why he was there and she could sneak out to work from home in the afternoon. No one at the paper seemed to care where she worked as long as she was accessible on her phone and met her deadlines. It was one of the few perks of journalism.

She got Olly settled with a coloring book and a box of crayons at one of the generic desks in the corner of the communication offices, then went in search of Captain Sinner. It had been two weeks since she'd first asked him about the incident. Now that several new witnesses had come forward to claim they'd seen the king and Mrs. Burnham ducking into her tent, she wanted to try again for a statement; running the article without it would make the case seem uninvestigated. She caught him in the hallway; he wasn't hard to spot with his neatly coiffed blond hair and striking blue eyes, standing a bit taller than the rest . . . not that Brooke noticed his looks.

"Good morning, Captain."

"Good morning, Ms. . . ."

"Everleigh," she said with a smile, suspecting that he already knew.

"Oh, that's right. I apologize, I can be so forgetful sometimes."

"Captain, would His Majesty like to comment on another recent statement from Greta Burnham, where she alleges that he manipulated her with . . ." Brooke's voice trailed off as she noticed Olly standing next to her. "Darling, go back and sit down where Mum showed you in the office, all right?"

"Who's this?" Saint asked, his tone light.

"I'm Oliver Charles Everleigh."

Saint stuck out his hand, and her son shook it. "Very nice to meet you, Oliver Charles Everleigh. I'm Captain Saint." He glanced at Brooke. "Is this your brother?"

She shook her head. "My son."

He gave her a single slow nod. "And are you sick today, Oliver Charles Everleigh?"

Her boy blushed. *Good. Be embarrassed.*

"No. School kicked me out for fighting on the playground."

"Oh, I see. Soldiers don't abide such behavior, either. A friend of mine was just demoted for such things."

Brooke swiped her phone open. "What friend?"

He gave her a quelling look. "Respectfully, I wasn't speaking to you, Ms. Everleigh. Now, what were you asking?"

"I was asking about the recent demotion of one of His Majesty's closest friends . . ."

He smirked. "I didn't say he was a friend of *Edward's*. I said he was a friend of *mine*. And I don't comment on my friends. Next question."

"Want to see my loose tooth?" This question, of course, came from Olly, who had not gone back to the office as requested.

"Sure." Saint bent down, squinting into Olly's small mouth.

Seriously? Brooke felt herself bristle that he was being so accommodating with her son and so impossible with her.

"Wow, that's something, all right. Bet it'll come out right quick." He stood and turned to her again. "No, His Majesty would not like to comment on Ms. Burnham's very grown-up statement that cannot be discussed in front of small ears."

"Would His Majesty like to comment on the statement of two Orangiersian officers who claim they witnessed Mrs. Burnham's awakening?"

"No, he would not."

"Would he like to offer any information about his whereabouts on the day in question?"

"No."

"Would he be willing to participate in an interview with—"

"Ms. Everleigh," Saint sighed. "You're chasing a dead end here. His Majesty is a decent man. He doesn't . . ." He glanced down at Olly's upturned face. "He doesn't have any magical ability, inclination, or interest, frankly. Moreover, His Majesty is a family man. He doesn't . . ." He glanced down at Olly again. "He is faithful to his wife. He was engaged to the grand duchess at that time."

"On the day in question, His Majesty had neither seen nor spoken to his fiancée in five years. Are we meant to believe that he was singularly focused on her during all that time?"

"The . . . *behavior* you're suggesting took place would not only be unseemly and inappropriate but would go against his character." He leaned closer to her. "Off the record?"

She nodded.

"Off the record, why the jack—"

"Jackrabbit," she quickly corrected, tipping her head toward Olly.

"Yes, sorry. Why the *jackrabbit* would His Majesty try to manipulate someone like that?"

"Power. Control. Thinks he can get away with it. She saw something he didn't want seen. Shall I go on?"

"What are you guys talking about?" Olly asked, pushing between them.

Brooke stuffed her annoyance. "Grown-up stuff, love. This is my work, remember? Asking hard questions?"

He seemed to consider this. "I'm gonna go play the computer."

"No. No games when you're suspended."

Olly's face reddened. "What?" he shouted. "You didn't tell me that! That's not fair!"

Brooke reddened, too. People around them fell silent to watch the confrontation. *Great.*

Saint crossed his arms. "Oliver, what do you want to be when you grow up?"

The boy's shoulders whipped back. "A soldier."

"Really?" He rubbed his chin. "Then you've got to learn to listen to your commanding officer. Do you know who that is?"

He shook his head. Saint pointed at Brooke, and Olly sneered.

"See, that attitude is no good. No man wants to go into battle with a man who can't follow orders. You can bet that I follow my commanding officer's orders. Every time. That's why he depends on me, gives me good duty like this instead of scrubbing bogs." He leaned over and his voice dropped. "But if he told me to scrub bogs, I'd do that, too, and it'd be the cleanest bog in Orangiers." He stood up. "You learn some discipline, and you could be a good soldier someday. But right now, you're not there."

Brooke's mouth fell open. *Why is he saying all this?* Olly looked devastated, and a flare of motherly protection surged inside her. "Now, Captain, don't . . ."

Saint kept his focus on Olly. "What did your CO ask you to do?"

"Go sit in the office," Olly mumbled.

"Go on, then. Quick now."

Olly turned and hurried down the hall. She'd tried everything lately to get him to obey . . . Was this all it took? Treating him like a soldier? She vacillated between frustration that Saint had gotten him to follow orders so quickly and shock that he'd backed her up.

"Did you need anything else from me?" Saint acted like nothing unusual had happened. She shook her head, still stunned.

"No, um, thank you. That's all."

"Have a nice day, Ms. Everleigh."

As it happened, she did not have a nice day. Between trying to keep Olly quiet, the stares she was getting from her other colleagues, Captain Saint's stonewalling, and the useless morning briefing, she gave up around eleven. After lunch, she took Olly to the park and worked on her laptop for a few hours on a metal park bench. Not that there was really that much to report yet; she just needed to keep after the story, she reminded herself. No one said it was going to be easy.

Brooke's phone rang: it was Greta. She skipped the pleasantries.

"I thought the story would've come out by now, Ms. Everleigh."

Though the woman couldn't see her, Brooke nodded. "I thought so, too. But we're still gathering information and testimonies, giving the king a chance to respond to the accusation. These things take time, I'm afraid." Her editor, Miranda, was dragging her feet a bit, which surprised Brooke, as this paper seemed to have a nose for scandal.

"I see." Even in those two words, there was an edge to her voice that made Brooke frown. But when she spoke again, it was gone. "It's just been hard waiting for all this to come out. I'm on pins and needles, just waiting. My reputation is at stake here."

"I understand. I'm doing all I can, Mrs. Burnham."

Olly came running over, red-faced, with an older black-haired boy close behind, and Brooke held up her hand for quiet. They both obeyed.

"Just please let me know when it will be out, won't you? I don't want to be blindsided."

"Yes, I will. I can certainly do that." They said their goodbyes, and Brooke sighed. "Thank you for waiting. Yes, love?"

"This kid lost his dog. Can we help him look?"

"Oh, of course. And let's ask him his name, shall we, rather than calling him 'this kid'?"

She tucked her notes into her bag and tried to think of something she could microwave for dinner, provided her microwave was working; it had been temperamental lately, and she didn't have the money to call a technician. "Where shall we start?" After forty minutes of tromping through Rogers Woods with Omar, they found Tagine sniffing around the entrance of a rabbit burrow and saw them both safely home.

At least today had a happy ending for someone.

CHAPTER FIVE

AS IT HAPPENED, THE day he met Olly wasn't a happy one for Saint, either. Saint was walking home when his brother called.

"Hey. What's up?"

His brother switched to Imaharan. "Mum's trying to set me up again. Talk to her for me."

Saint chuckled and replied in Imaharan. "Hinata, just tell her no."

"You know I can't do that. I don't know how it's so easy for you."

"Such a good son," Saint teased. "You go have lunch with that medical transcriptionist with the wide hips, good for childbearing."

Hinata's tone was haughty. "She's a receptionist in a real estate office and her hips are average size."

"Her parents are Imaharan, I assume?"

"Yes. But I don't mind that." As far as Saint could tell, Hinata didn't mind any of it. He just needed a reason to call; he wasn't the type to just phone for a chat. Complaining about Mum was a safe pretext, since he knew Saint wouldn't actually come to his defense in the matter.

"Girls come in all flavors, you know."

"Don't be crude. It will make them happy if she's Imaharan." And with his dark hair, constant smile, and unusual height for an Imaharan, Hinata was a catch.

"Then why don't you want to go?"

"I don't want to get married yet. I'd like to breathe a little before I dive into a new relationship. But Mum thinks now that I have the restaurant open, I'm successful and it'll be easier to find me a wife."

"Has she not been to the restaurant to see how much work it is?"

"She doesn't like fusion. When I did the preview event, she said my recipes were 'sadly nontraditional.'"

Saint chuckled. "No one throws shade like Mum." His phone beeped to indicate another call coming in, and he checked the screen. His mood darkened immediately.

"Hinata, it's Calynda calling. I should probably answer."

"Okay, brother. See you soon."

"Yep." He touched the screen to answer. "Hello?"

"Baby? It's me, Mum."

He hadn't called her Mum for years; his adoptive mum—his *real* mum—was a petite black-haired woman who had him completely wrapped around her little finger by virtue of her persistent, gentle love for him. In the fourteen years since he'd joined her family, she'd never tried to manipulate him. She'd never needed to.

"Hello, Calynda. What can I do for you?"

"Can't you at least call me Mum?" she whined, and he suppressed an eye roll, even though she couldn't see him.

"What can I do for you, Calynda?"

"It's not my fault, baby, but I'm in kind of a tight spot financially this month. Can you float me a loan? Just for a few weeks until my settlement check comes."

He almost admired her true dedication to the fiction she concocted about her own life. *Float* sounded like such an innocent word. It was assuredly her fault. Her lawsuit wasn't going to pan out—he'd spoken to her lawyer, who'd admitted as much—considering the jury suspected that it hadn't been a coincidence or an accident that the driver of the car hit her, even if she'd made it appear that way. If he was a betting man, he'd wager she was already injured when she entered the crosswalk.

"I'd like to remind you that I already floated you a loan last month which has yet to float back in my direction."

"Oh, it will, baby. I'm so close to making it."

"Uh-huh." It was a struggle to keep his tone kind. "How much?"

"Just $1,000. No, $1,500." Someone next to her had upped the ask. A man's voice.

"Who've you got there with you?"

"Just a friend. He's been helping me out, letting me stay at his place . . ."

"Then why am I paying for rent on an apartment for you?"

"Oh, that place didn't work out, I haven't been there for a while."

She's using. Again. That's the only reason he could imagine that it wouldn't have worked out. He was surprised the landlord hadn't called him to complain. Probably just easier to threaten to turn her in and keep collecting his money.

"I can give you $800." *It's what I would've spent on rent, anyway.*

"Oh, Franny, you're such a good son. Thank you, sweetheart. This is just temporary, you know."

"Right." It'd been the temporary situation for ten years now, ever since he'd reconnected with Calynda during a phase of teenage angst over his identity. It wasn't that he didn't care about her at all, but his love was tired.

"I'll come to the palace to pick it up."

Saint scowled. "No, I'll meet you at the train station." He wasn't surprised that she knew where he worked, but he wasn't about to let her in the front doors of Bluffton. He'd leave the family tours to Ms. Everleigh. Why she thought it was appropriate to bring a child to work was beyond him. *She'll probably be gone soon, anyway.*

"Oh, I don't mind."

"Calynda. I'll meet you at the train station near Bluffton at seven."

"When am I going to get to see your new place, baby?"

Never. The last thing I need is you and your man of the moment knocking on my door at all hours.

"Not this week. See you at seven." Saint hung up. He lashed out at a low-hanging branch, and the brown leaves went flying. He knew what would happen at seven. She'd try to touch his cheeks, and the guy she was with would hang around and smoke and try not to make eye contact so he'd be harder to identify from a lineup later. She'd cry and be grateful, so grateful for her good, good son. She'd make promises, both big and small: "I'll get this back to you real soon. I'll call you tomorrow." But then she *couldn't* . . . There was always a reason.

Saint felt sick; he was going to need some serious time with his drum set tonight. Maybe he'd stop by the Rusty Nail for a drink, too. Woz, he was so glad she wasn't his real mum. If she hadn't gotten caught for possession of pirate powder, she'd have probably raised him in this jacked-up environment his whole life.

CHAPTER SIX

"MRS. EVERLEIGH, THANK you for coming," the school's principal said as she shut the door. Brooke was tired of correcting her, so she let the "Mrs." slide. "How are you today?"

"I'm fine." In fact, she'd responded to the midnight call of a frantic neighbor who wanted to know if she had any infant acetaminophen. She'd stayed up with Sarah for an hour, waiting to see if the medicine was working or if she'd need to wake Olly and take everyone to urgent care. She'd been by herself too many times to allow this young mama to do that alone.

The woman stared at her expectantly as she sat behind the desk, but Brooke had nothing more to say. She knew she should try to charm these people; it would be painful for them both if Olly got kicked out of kindergarten. This was a nice school, in general . . . and it was close to her apartment.

Mrs. Foster cleared her throat. "Our school has a zero-tolerance policy when it comes to violence, as you know. That being said, Oliver is quite young, and we understand that disputes do happen between young children."

Brooke let out a breath she didn't realize she'd been holding.

"For an older child, we might recommend some kind of community service or chores to benefit the school community . . . but when I spoke to Oliver earlier today, it seemed like there might be a more productive solution, a more profitable solution for everyone."

"Okay . . . What does that mean?"

The woman's eyes dropped to her desk, and she fidgeted with a pen, lining it up with a stack of books. "We'd like to assign Oliver a mentor. Someone to form a positive attachment with him, outside of school. Just for a few months, until it seems like he's settled."

Brooke resisted the impulse to cross her arms. "I see. And who is this mentor?"

The principal looked up and smiled. "Here he is now." The door behind her opened, and Brooke turned to look into the face of Captain Saint. His cold gaze bounced between her face and the principal's.

"Ms. Everleigh." His voice held a note of surprise.

"You remembered my name after all. Interesting."

"Not difficult to do when it keeps crossing my desk, each question more ridiculous than the last."

"Can I quote you on that?"

"No, you may not." He looked at the stunned woman behind the desk. "Mrs. Foster, may I speak with you in private?"

The principal followed him out into the hallway. Brooke could only catch snatches of their conversation . . . "That woman." "Impossible." "Responsible." "Promised."

They filed back into the room, both looking unhappy, and took their seats. "So," Mrs. Foster said, grimacing, "from what I understand, you already know each other, and it's not under the best of circumstances. But it really shouldn't affect Oliver's participation in the program. You won't be spending much time together, just the captain and Oliver."

"No. Absolutely not. This donkey is not going to influence my kid; he's a total womanizer."

"Mrs. Everleigh, let's keep things civil."

"Ms."

The two women looked at Captain Saint simultaneously.

"Pardon?" the principal said.

"It's *Ms.* Everleigh," he corrected again. "Right?"

"Yes," Brooke answered, baffled. "I apologize if my state-ment came off as uncivil, but I have some deep concerns about this pairing. Isn't there anyone else?"

Mrs. Foster shook her head, removing her glasses. "We're short on mentors, especially this late in the year; we usually pair the students and mentors in Eighth Month, and here it is Ninth Month already. Captain Saint had been paired with an-other student, but she recently moved away. If you choose not to take advantage of this opportunity, we'll have to make Oliv-er's expulsion permanent, I'm afraid."

"What?" Brooke felt her knees shaking; this was what she was afraid of. Her heart sank like a stone.

"As I said, it's a zero-tolerance policy."

"With all due respect, Principal Foster, they were just fight-ing over a toy. That's what kids do."

"The wound Oliver inflicted on the other boy required stitches, Ms. Everleigh. This was no basic playground squab-ble." She leaned forward. "Please understand, we want Olly here. Most of the time, he's a very sweet boy, and when I ob-served him in class, it seemed like he's starting to build some friendships. I'd hate for him to lose that."

Brooke was chewing on her bottom lip so hard, she was pretty sure it was going to start bleeding any minute. The woman wasn't wrong; he'd come home just the other day with a story about a boy named Harry, who shared his crayons with Olly. Art had always been the way to her boy's heart . . . Maybe

Harry could be a buddy for him. He needed that. She could always supervise them herself if she was concerned.

"Look," Saint said gruffly, "when I met him at Bluffton, he seemed like a nice enough kid. It's just for a few months. It'll be fine."

She pivoted to glare at him. "Gee, I don't remember asking for your opinion, but thanks."

"Ms. Everleigh, Captain Saint is one of our most experienced mentors. I promise your son will be in good hands with him. I personally guarantee it."

"I want to supervise their meetings. At least the first few."

The principal glanced at the man next to her, who gave a single nod. "Fine. It's a deal. I'll leave it to you to exchange contact information and set up your first meeting."

"Fine. Thank you, Mrs. Foster." Brooke grabbed her purse off the floor and hurried out of the office and down the hall.

"Hey!"

A glance over her shoulder confirmed her suspicions: he was following her.

Brooke whirled on him. "How did you work this out? Does it make you feel superior, trying to punish me?"

"Me?" he growled. "What makes you think I'm any happier about this than you are?"

"Because it causes me pain, Captain. I'm pretty sure that's high on your list of things to do."

"To the contrary, Ms. Everleigh. Officially, I have nothing but the best of intentions toward you or any other member of the press."

"Officially?"

He grinned, sliding his oversized sunglasses onto the bridge of his nose, popping a piece of gum into his mouth. "Officially, yes."

She leaned closer to his smug face. "What about unofficially?"

"I don't think I should discuss that."

"Shocker." She started down the hall again. "You can meet us at Rogers Park tonight at 5:30."

He fell into step with her. *Darn these short legs.* "I usually come to the child's home . . ."

"You take one step into my house, and I will call the police to arrest you for trespassing." She would abide no abusers in her home, and if he was covering for Edward, that made him culpable.

"Come on, it's cold outside. You'd rather come to my house?"

"Where is it?"

"533 Yarrow Place, West Cheekton." She put it into her phone's map. That was just under a mile from her apartment. They could walk that pretty easily. She'd probably have to drag Olly home afterward, when he was tired and ready for bed, but it was doable. Maybe they'd take the train home—it would be dark.

"Fine. We'll be there at 5:45. We'll stay for an hour."

"See you then."

She paused and he strode past her toward the double doors of the school. The feeling of having misbehaved nagged at her.

"Wait," she blurted out.

Saint turned, mostly silhouetted against the sunny fall day outside.

"Can I bring anything?"

"Yeah, bring yourself a salad. I hear mums like salad." He smirked, opening the door with his back. Brooke stood in the hallway trying to breathe instead of scream for a few seconds before she went outside to catch the train back to the newspaper offices.

TWENTY MINUTES LATE, they turned onto Yarrow Place. Olly's initial enthusiasm to spend time with Captain Saint had worn off about half a mile into their walk, and now he was whining incessantly about being out in the dark and missing his evening screen time. Brooke dragged him the last block by his right hand and took a deep breath before she knocked on the door.

"Ms. Everleigh."

"Captain."

"Take your shoes off, please. Good evening, Oliver. How's the loose tooth?"

"Almost out now," he mumbled, suddenly distracted by his own mouth's contents. "See?" He pushed it forward with his tongue and Brooke opened her mouth to correct him.

"You can go sit in the living room, Ms. Everleigh."

Dismissed. Like a good subordinate. It took serious effort not to huff her annoyance . . . especially when she saw what they were eating for dinner. *Pepperoni pizza? On a weeknight?* She usually saved treats like that for weekends and hoped it wouldn't give Olly something new to complain about.

"You've got a *dog*?" Olly rushed to the glass door and pressed his face against it. The large brown short-hair pressed his nose right back, barking twice.

"Yes, that's Buster. He's still kind of a puppy, so he gets a little too excited when there's new people. Maybe you can play with him next time."

Olly's grin was wide as he slid into a chair at the kitchen table.

"So," Captain Saint deadpanned, "do you like pizza?"

He nodded eagerly, and Saint passed him a piece.

"Where's the plates?" Brooke asked, looking around.

Captain Saint shrugged. "We men don't need them, do we? Just keep the grease on the table, eh?"

Brooke rolled her eyes so hard, she could actually feel her optic nerves straining. She opened her mouth to protest, but the captain gave her a hard look that had her mouth snapping shut again. She pulled out her laptop and opened it. The Wi-Fi icon popped up, and she clicked on it. *Password required.* Rather than yell across the room, Brooke got up and shuffled through the open-concept living room to the kitchen.

"Sorry to interrupt. Can I get the Wi-Fi password?"

"Sorry, no. It's very long and complicated and I can't remember it. I'm busy with Olly right now." He turned back to Olly. "And then what did Ultraman do?"

"He was like BAM! BAM! And then Wolfwoman tried to get up, but he was like SLAM, and she couldn't."

"Not sure I approve of anyone who beats up a woman like that, mate."

"No, but she's wicked," Olly explained seriously. "She's wicked."

"Even wicked women deserve a little respect," Saint said, sliding his gaze to Brooke in challenge.

Oh, you think you're so clever . . . donkey. Brooke spun on her heel and went back to the living room, pulling out the book she'd brought, turning to face the unlit fireplace, the kitchen at her back. It was literary historical fiction, and she'd been trying to get into it for a few nights now, but she kept falling asleep after a few paragraphs. Tonight, she was too distracted.

"How's school going, mate?"

"Good," Olly said, his mouth still full of pizza. "Can I have more?"

Is that his third piece? I hope he doesn't make himself sick.

"Yeah? What's the best thing that happened today?"

"I don't know."

"Okay. You think for a moment, and I'll tell you my best thing while you're thinking. Deal?"

Olly must've nodded, because Saint went on. "Let's see . . . Well, my best thing was probably going to the batting cages with my friend James. Do you like baseball?"

"Yup."

"Me too. I could use some advice, though . . . My friend James wasn't too good at hitting the ball. What should I say to James, do you think, if he just can't seem to connect with the ball?"

"Maybe just say, 'Go Team Everleigh,' or something."

"Team Everleigh? What's that?" She heard the surprise in his voice and felt herself blush.

Olly spoke through his food again, and Brooke cringed at his manners. "That's Mum and me. And Gran sometimes.

We're Team Everleigh. That's how we cheer at video games and football. I like the bike racing game."

"Oh, me too—like when you take a controller in each hand and they go up and down faster and faster, only you can't go up the hill too fast or he tips over?"

They laughed together, and Brooke relaxed a little bit. *Mrs. Foster was right. This will be okay. I don't have to like him for Olly to like him.* She snuggled into the couch, letting the book fall to her chest for a moment. The next thing she knew, someone was flicking her ear. Hard.

"Hey!" She flinched away, and Saint chuckled into his fist. She glared at him. "I thought we were keeping it civil."

"He's in the bathroom. This was my chance."

"Probably with a stomachache from too much pizza. Thanks so much for that."

"Aww, you're welcome," he said warmly, as if he hadn't caught her sarcasm. "It was my pleasure."

"Ugh." Brooke raised her voice, as she stuffed her belongings back in her messenger bag, smashing the salad she'd brought but not eaten. "Olly, love, let's go, it's getting late." She checked her phone—7:30. *Sugar, he should be in bed already.* They'd have to take the train now. *More money gone.* "Super late. Come on, kid." Olly came running down the hall, and she quickly got him into his coat and shoes. "Say thank you to Captain Saint."

"Thanks, Captain." He looked up. "Mum, you're drooling."

Saint looked away, smirking. She swiped at the corner of her mouth and squared her shoulders.

"Great. Well, we'll see you next week."

"Nope. You'll see me tomorrow. Can't get all the hours in without meeting several times a week, and we're already behind."

"Behind? Behind who? Is everything a competition with you?" She could hear the acid in her own voice, and she blamed being rudely awoken.

He glared at her. "Behind the other participants in the mentoring program. It's a set schedule."

"Oh." It was on the tip of her tongue to apologize, but she couldn't quite bring herself to do it. "Well, unfortunately, we're busy tomorrow." It was a complete lie, but she was exhausted. *I'm not doing this again tomorrow.*

"Fine. Friday, then."

"Oh!" Olly cried. "Can Captain Saint come to our house this time? And he can play bike riding with us? Please, Mum?"

NO. JERSEY, NO. NO TIMES A MILLION.

"Sure," she bit out insincerely. "Give me your phone number, and I'll text you on Friday." He kept his eyes on her face as he reached around her and pulled the phone out of her back pocket, making her jump. Brooke felt her face redden. "What are you doing?"

He raised an eyebrow. "Giving you my phone number?"

She crossed her arms. "Next time, you'll ask before you take anything out of my pockets."

"Yes, ma'am," he said, smirking.

Always smirking. I wonder if he'd smirk if I slapped him right across his smug face. Her hand quivered with the overwhelming desire to try it and see. He handed her back her phone. She looked at his entry.

"'*Captain* Saint'? You don't have a first name?"

"Captain's fine." He turned to Olly. "Good night, mate. See you Friday." He held up his hand too high for a high five, and Olly jumped to reach it. "Oh, good one."

Brooke threw open the front door, relieved to feel the cool evening air on her face again. *The first step toward home, my pajamas, and my knitting.* Olly would follow her. He was magnetized to her.

"Oh dear. Your mum's forgotten her manners again. Good night, Ms. Everleigh!" he called after her too loudly. She waved over her shoulder and heard Olly's footsteps running to catch up with her. "Have a wonderful evening! It was lovely to have you in my home!" Saint yelled. "I look forward to doing it again soon!" As soon as Olly passed her, she flipped Saint off without looking back and heard his answering laugh. Then she bent to let Olly climb on her back and felt him relax as her even steps rocked him home.

CHAPTER SEVEN

"THIS LETHOSIAN SALAD is so good. I love feta."

"Mmm." Her mother pushed her pasta around her plate, twirling her fork, then sloughing the spiral off on the side of her plate. Outside, the wind was picking up, swirling crispy leaves in the gutters of downtown Barrowdon; rain looked imminent. Brooke loved this kind of weather, for this kind of weather meant the holidays were coming. She already had a Christmas countdown going, even though it wasn't for three months.

"It's got black olives, too. And they actually left off the chicken like I asked them to, unlike the employees in the food truck near my office, who don't seem to understand vegetarianism whatsoever. They act like it's an affront to their culinary creations. I just don't like it! I'm not trying to offend them."

"Right."

Brooke wiped a drip of the citrusy dressing off her chin with her napkin, watching her mum warily. "Mum."

"Yes?"

"Everything all right?" She came by her oversharing naturally; one of her crueler boyfriends had called it verbal diarrhea. She preferred to think of it as a waterfall of ideas, but either way, she'd learned it from her mother. They usually barely ate anything at these lunches, they were so busy sharing articles, recipes, stories of what happened on the train or at work. Today, her mother could barely make eye contact with her, and she was shaking the table with her knee, which hadn't ceased bouncing since she sat down.

She gave her a weak smile. "Of course."

"How's your week going?"

"Fine." She lifted her half-full fork to her mouth, then set it back down.

"What's wrong with it?"

"Nothing."

"We can always send it back. You know how I love dealing with unreasonable waitstaff." It wasn't sarcasm. If people needed to battle their cable company over an incorrect bill or confront a repairman over a botched job, she took it on with relish.

"No, the food's fine."

"Okay."

Brooke looked around the restaurant, then up at the inset speakers in the ceiling. "Deck the Walls" was playing, and she grinned. "It's started, Mum. This is my first Christmas song in public for the season." She waited for her mother to begin her rant about how it started earlier and earlier every year and how it diluted the holiday to play Christmas music all year (like Brooke did). Theresa just smiled.

Confused, Brooke focused on her salad, trying to spear the perfect ratio of cheese to tomatoes, peppers, and cucumbers, while avoiding the raw onion. Her phone dinged, and she automatically pulled it out of her purse.

"You're going to answer it?" The hurt in her mother's expression surprised her.

"You're not even talking, Mom; can you blame me? My job's a lot more demanding now. Plus, Olly's had so many problems lately, it could be the school."

Her mother nodded, clearly not buying it, and Brooke read the text message from her editor.

Miranda: Greta Burnham to take the polygraph next Friday at 2:00. Palace is sending representatives to observe. Barrowdon City Hall.

Brooke: I'll be there.

Miranda: Great.

"Good news?" her mom asked quietly.

Brooke nodded. "Great news. There's going to be an investigation into my story, the Greta Burnham thing?"

"That's great, Brooke." She wiped her mouth with her napkin and put it over her plate, despite not having eaten a bite.

Brooke set down her fork and put her arms on the table, leaning forward. "If you don't tell me what's wrong, I'm going to write your phone number on the bathroom stall in the men's room at the Rusty Nail, indicating that you're up for a good time."

"I'm moving, honey."

Her gourmet salad turned to sawdust in her mouth. "You're what?"

"I'm moving. To Gardenia. Your grandmother needs me there all the time. I can't keep going back and forth, it's too hard."

Brooke was silent, her brain spinning. *What? Um, what? Also, what?* Okay, so it was kind of recycling that one thought . . . but it was the only one it could reach.

"Why can't you bring Nana here?"

"She's lived in that house her whole life. I can't ask her to leave, it would kill her."

"What about me and Olly?"

Her mother covered her face with her hands. "I know," she said, her fingers muffling the sound of her voice. "I'm sorry. I have to do this, Brooke. She's my mom."

"Why is this the first I'm hearing of this? You're moving across the continent, and you never thought to pick up the phone and be like, 'Hey, daughter, I'm considering this huge life change . . .'"

"I've been thinking about it for a while," Theresa said, reaching for her wine glass and downing half of it in one swig.

The day drinking is starting to make more sense.

"So again, I'm wondering why you didn't say anything . . ."

"Stop interrogating me, Brooke. This is happening. I'm putting my house on the market next weekend, and I need you to come over and get your stuff out of the guest bedroom." Her mom knocked back the rest of her wine, and Brooke reached out to cover her hand with her own.

"Mom. I'm not interrogating. I'm just asking. I'm just super confused." Brooke fought a feeling of betrayal; she'd thought this would be the kind of thing her mother would want her opinion on, the kind of thing they'd tackle together. It wasn't just that she was leaving; it was that she'd planned and executed it apart from her involvement entirely.

Teresa's bottom lip trembled. "I know. I'm sorry. I should've spoken to you earlier. I just . . . I just knew you'd be upset."

She squeezed her hand. "I am upset. I'm very upset. But I'm mostly sad you thought I wouldn't support you. You know how much we love you; of course we'll support you. You've been there for me for a long time, and I understand if you need to take care of Nana." *Even if it's really, really screwing up my life*.

. . She wouldn't think about it now. Even across the café table, Brooke could see her mom's eyes were brimming with tears.

"Thank you, love. Thank you for understanding."

Brooke looked toward the door. "Do you want to get out of here?"

"So much." They both grabbed their purses and went up front to pay. "I've got to finish up at work and get home and clean. Olly invited *him* over to play video games and eat pizza."

Teresa put her hand to her chest. "He's crashing your pizza night? Is nothing sacred?"

"I know!" Brooke threw up her hands in exasperation before she caught her mother's almost-not-there smirk. "Oh, you're hilarious." A wave of grief hit Brooke. She wasn't going to be able to leave work to take a long lunch with her mother anymore. "I'll come get that stuff on Wednesday." She let one tear fall. Then she got back on the train to hurry downtown again.

CHAPTER EIGHT

SAINT: What time shall I be at your nest?

    Brooke: My nest?

    Saint: Yes, a viper lives in a nest, doesn't it?

    Brooke: Does it hurt?

    Saint: What?

    Brooke: When your knuckles drag on the ground.

    Brooke: 5:30.

    Saint: Address?

    Brooke: 54612 E. Farlight, Apt. 416

    Saint: Elevator?

    Brooke: Be a man, for Woz's sake.

    Saint: Men invented elevators.

Brooke jammed her phone into her back pocket and set about kneading the pizza dough. It was taking longer than usual, since she had to make an extra pizza. At least she wouldn't have to worry about lunch for Olly tomorrow; she could work a little longer that way. Brooke got out her mandoline slicer and cut the zucchini into thin, even rounds, keeping her mind on her cooking lest she remove the end of her finger accidentally. She chopped the spinach and roma tomatoes, and Olly appeared at her side as if by magic. She tossed a tomato hunk to him, and he caught it in his mouth, grinning, then went back to whatever imaginary game he'd been playing down the hall. *That kid loves vegetables.* She had just added the peppers to the hot pan to sauté, when she heard someone knock forcefully across the hall. A moment later, she heard Mr. Fredrick-

46

son yelling, "Can't you read, young man? It says 'No soliciting.' I don't want whatever you're selling! Leave me alone!" *Slam.* A moment later, her phone plinked.

Saint: You said 416.

Brooke: Oh, did I? Fingers must've slipped.

Brooke: It's 418.

There was a knock, somewhat more hesitant this time, at her own door, and she snickered before she called out, "Oliver! Your guest is here."

Her boy came tearing through the apartment.

"No running, kiddo. Mrs. Cavanaugh doesn't like that, remember?"

He slowed down and threw the door open. "Captain Saint!"

"Olly!" He mirrored the kid's enthusiasm so genuinely that she had to remind herself that it wasn't. That kind of man didn't like kids. Not really. "Is this your place, mate?" Saint toed off his shoes and loosened his tie, and Brooke tried not to notice how it softened the man's intimidating appearance.

"Yup, this is our house," he said proudly. Brooke winced a little; a house it wasn't. Technically, his bedroom wasn't even a bedroom . . . It had no windows and probably wasn't legal, but it was cheap.

"Do you want to see my room?"

Brooke opened her mouth to protest, but Saint cut her off. "Just for a minute, sure." When they turned the corner down the hall to the bedrooms, Brooke crept to the edge of the living room to listen to their conversation.

"And these are my Karate Kats."

"Uh-huh," Saint said.

"And this is the picture I drew with Rachel. It's an octopus."

"Nice. Why'd you make it purple?"

"They really are purple," Olly explained, and she wasn't surprised by his ardent sincerity.

"Are they?" Saint sounded skeptical, but didn't argue with him. Which was smart, because Olly was obsessed with the ocean. Before they started back, she tiptoed into the kitchen and slid the first pizza into the oven. Something buzzed, and she turned. It buzzed again: Saint had left his phone on the kitchen island, and it was ringing: *Calynda Huxley.* Probably some bimbo he'd gone out with, but you never knew where a story was going to come from. If he was covering up Edward's indiscretions, perhaps he had some of his own. Maybe she could extend her coverage of the story. She made a mental note of the name just as they came back into the room.

"Dinnertime?" Olly asked.

"Not yet. A few more minutes. Do you want to get your scooter and go across to the park? Captain Saint really likes going up and down our stairs."

Olly's freckled nose crinkled. "You do? I hate it."

"So do I," Captain Saint assured him, glaring at Brooke. "Do you have any homework?"

"Just reading a book."

"Get one. Let's do it."

Olly's eyes were wide. "But it's Friday. I don't have to do it until Sunday night."

Saint sat down on their plaid thrift store couch. "Well, there's two ways to look at it. One: you can let it hang over your head all weekend. Two: you can do it now and relax until Monday."

Olly kicked at the carpet. "I think I'll wait until Sunday."

Saint leaned forward onto his knees. "Would you like to choose the book, or shall I?"

Scowling a little, Olly trudged off to his room, and Saint pivoted to her.

"Where'd you order from? I know I'll hate it, but tell me anyway."

"I didn't order it," she said, wiping down the counters. "I made it."

"She cooks. Amazing you haven't given up mudslinging to be someone's little wifey."

"First of all, I don't cook. I bake. There's a difference. And second . . ."

Olly came running back in, and Brooke didn't bother asking him to walk again; he was too excited. She'd just take Mrs. Cavanaugh another plate of cookies to apologize for the noise. Of the six flavors she'd tried so far, the molasses cookies seemed to pacify the old woman the most.

"Who reads this?" Saint asked Olly. "You or me?"

"You," Olly laughed. "I don't read."

"You don't read *yet*. Yet's a powerful word, mate. You'll read soon enough. Just wait and see. You'll be learning your letters, learning your sounds, then suddenly, BAM! Reading."

Brooke almost wished he was worse at this. His competency with her son was . . . annoying. And yet, she could see that Saint's magic was working on Olly. Her son was riveted by the superhero story—the captain even did voices. *But I do them better.*

"You do the voices better than Mum." *Oh. I guess not.* Brooke turned her back to the pair lest she have to endure some kind of belittling from Saint. Having him here was . . . awkward. This was one of the few nights she took off to be with Olly in more than just "get it done" mothering mode. It wasn't his fault . . . but she still didn't like it. And yet, watching him read to Olly . . . he obviously had a way with kids. She wasn't eager to re-examine her initial impressions of the man, but . . .

Her phone timer trilled and she pulled the first pizza out and put the second one in.

The males gravitated toward her, sniffing.

"What the . . ." Saint's voice trailed off as he swallowed his curse words in light of Olly's presence. "What's on this, mate?"

"All kinds of good veggies. Mum makes the best pizza in the world," Olly said, carrying the plates to the table as Brooke passed them to him.

Saint grunted, swiping his phone off the island. A moment later, her pocket dinged.

Saint: You did this to punish me, didn't you?

Brooke: Don't flatter yourself.

Saint: Just admit it.

Brooke: Sorry to disappoint.

Brooke: Heaven forbid we make a decision based on our needs rather than yours.

Saint: You're a vegetarian? What am I saying, of course you're a vegetarian.

Saint: I refuse to call something a pizza that doesn't have meat on it.

Brooke: You are ridiculous.

They both sat down at the table, him glaring, her smiling. Olly helped himself to a slice of pizza, oblivious as usual, and Brooke served the adult plates.

Saint poked cautiously at the piece she served him. "Big plans this weekend, mate?"

"Mum, do we have plans?"

"Just cleaning." She saved most of her household chores for weekends; if nothing else, it gave her a chance to get away from her computer and out of her own head. This weekend, she'd be picturing erasing Captain Sinner's annoying face as she scrubbed the soap scum in her shower.

"Sounds riveting," he said dryly.

"What about you, Captain? A big weekend of skirt chasing planned?"

"As a matter of fact, I don't have to chase them." He took a big bite of the pizza and talked through it. "They come to me."

"Of course they do."

"What does that mean, 'skirt chasing'?" Olly asked, also through his pizza.

"It means I like talking to women."

"Why did she say skirts, though?"

"Never mind," Brooke said. "Did you show Captain Saint your artwork?" Art was always the way to distract her kid.

He nodded eagerly. "The octopus."

"Oh, that one's my favorite," Brooke cooed. She loved that her kid was creative, even if it took a different bent than her own creative outlets. Her writing was sometimes more work than play, but the feeling of weaving words together, of painting a situation with nuance and care, that never got old. "Do you want me to get out the oil pastels?" She'd scored a deal on them at a garage sale over the summer.

"Yes, yes, yes!" Olly yelled.

"Yes, yes, yes!" Saint parroted, mimicking the excitement. "What's oil pastels?"

"You don't know? Olly asked, aghast, and ran over to the low cupboard where they kept the art supplies. Brooke moved quietly to the kitchen to put dinner away.

"You draw, too, Mum."

"Oh, um . . ." She'd planned to clean up, then retreat to her bedroom with her laptop to give them some time together.

"Sure, Mum can come draw with us," Saint said. His amused gaze told her that he'd known she wasn't planning to join them. "That's kind of you to invite her."

"Yes, very kind," she muttered, getting out the glass food storage containers. It was, actually. That was the trouble. Her kid was being sweet, and she felt guilty for resenting it. Brooke turned around and forced a smile. "Thanks, Ol, I'd love to draw with you."

She finished clearing the table, then joined them at the coffee table, opting to sit on the floor rather than on the couch next to Saint. She could still smell his cologne hanging in the air, and she tried to ignore it. She liked it.

"What are you drawing, son?" She felt self-conscious calling him her "sweet son" in front of the captain, even though that was his given nickname.

"A horse."

"Mmm, I can see it." She turned. "And you, Captain?"

"What does it look like?"

Is this a trap? It feels like a trap. "Uh, a sailboat?"

He scowled. "Not just any sailboat. Olly, what sailboat is this?"

Oliver glanced over, then shrugged.

"How are you raising this boy without him knowing the fastest schooner on the continent? That's the *Matilda Jane*! Three-time winner of the Schooner Classic Cup!"

Brooke smirked as she picked out a purple crayon. "Well, if I didn't know, it doesn't seem that essential. And the day they transfer me to sports is the day I quit."

"Shame on you, woman. This is part of his cultural history."

"Mum?" Olly asked, not looking up.

"No, pieces in the Orangiers Museum for Artistry in Diverse Mediums are part of his cultural history."

"We're a seafaring people, Everleigh. Don't try to make this about something else."

"Mum?" Olly asked again.

"Me? I'm not the one implying that we're not patriotic just because we don't follow competitive boating. Seriously, I don't get the appeal."

"Captain Saint—" Olly started, when he was interrupted.

"Just because *you* don't see the appeal doesn't mean it's not a worthwhile and beloved national pastime."

"So's alcoholism. Popularity does not automatically make something worth my time!"

"Based on your pizza toppings, your judgment is clearly not reliable."

"MUM!" Olly hollered over their bickering.

"What?" she snapped, then softened. "Sorry, Olly—what was it you needed?"

"I just want you guys to stop *fighting*." Now that she was looking at him, his chest was rising and falling faster than it should be. He looked like he might cry.

"Hey, buddy, we didn't mean to scare you." She reached out and pulled him into her side, kissing the top of his blond head. "The captain and I just like to . . . discuss things."

"You're not even drawing!" he protested, pointing at her blank page.

"Okay, okay, you're right, I'm sorry." She was a terrible artist. She always drew the same thing. She started the familiar outline of her chosen creature.

"What's that? A dog?" asked Saint, peering at the page.

"No," she said primly. "It's a penguin." Her third-grade teacher, Mrs. Blake, had taught her how to draw a good one, and she'd never forgotten it.

"Hmm," Captain Saint said, lifting an eyebrow, but said nothing more. After they'd completed drawings of three penguins, one sailboat, one dog, one house, one mountain landscape and one battlefield, Saint stood up. "I've got to get home and let Buster out."

Brooke felt her chest constrict, and knew she had to say something. "Olly, say good night to Captain Saint, then run and pick out a story, all right?"

They did their jumping high five, same as last time, then Olly ran down the hallway.

Brooke pushed the words out of her mouth before she could lose her nerve. "I want to thank you for working with Olly despite . . . everything. You have a way with him. So . . . thank you."

The smug look on his face was almost unbearable. "That must have been difficult for you to say."

"In fact, it was."

"Especially after the fuss you put up about me being selected . . ."

"Get out."

Saint grinned as he shrugged on his coat and left. After he was gone and Olly was tucked into bed, Brooke tried to warm a cold cup of tea in the microwave and ran a background check on the captain. The microwave groaned; she knew it wasn't really alive, but it sometimes felt that way. Veil Technology appliances weren't supposed to require cooperation to work like non-tech devices did, but sometimes, her microwave just seemed like it needed a hug. "Rough day?" she asked it, stroking the top of it, and it limped to life, its turntable jerkily rotating her blue mug, and it managed a lukewarm product. "Me too."

It couldn't hurt anything to run the background check . . . and it came back squeaky clean. *Good.* Then she remembered the name that had flashed on his phone . . . *What could it hurt to run her name, too?* He hadn't called the woman back right away, so maybe she wasn't important to him after all, but curiosity was nibbling at her mind.

CALYNDA MARIE HUXLEY

Married in the year 489, the ninth day of Sixth Month, to Jack S. Ryland. Divorced in the year 491, the third day of First Month.

Married in the year 491, the twelfth day of Third Month to Gregory Paul Trout. Divorced in the year 491, the twenty-fifth day of Eighth Month.

Married in the year 493, the first day of Tenth Month, to Daniel Jerome Saint. Divorced in the year 495, the fifth day of Tenth Month. The union produced one child, Francis Daniel

Saint, born in the year 493, the thirteenth day of Eleventh Month.

Brooke intended to stop reading there; she'd seen enough. This was his mum; she'd conceived him out of wedlock and then married his father briefly. This was his personal life, not his work life. She'd been nosy enough . . . but the criminal record heading was just too tempting.

Arrested for possession of an illegal substance in the year 490, the thirty-first of First Month. Released on probation in the year 490, the thirtieth of Fourth Month.

Arrested for violation of probation in the year 490, the twentieth of Twelfth Month. Released on parole the year 491, the second day of Second Month.

Arrested for possession of an illegal substance in the year 491, the twenty-first day of Ninth Month.

It read like a seesaw: Arrested, released. Arrested, released. Even after Saint—*Francis*—was born, she was in and out of jail. Then in the year 500, it changed: Calynda had gone away for three years, for dealing this time. *Who the Jersey was taking care of her kid? A grandmother, maybe?* It couldn't have been easy on him; he'd been seven years old. Sugar, no one deserved that kind of treatment.

Brooke closed the document, deciding that she didn't need to see any more. She didn't want to feel sorry for him. He was still kind of a jerk, whatever had happened to him when he was a kid. But when she imagined him in foster care, or worse, in whatever place Calynda had been living while she was using and dealing illegal substances . . . Brooke shuddered.

CHAPTER NINE

THE RUSTY NAIL WAS loud, even for a Saturday night. Judson leaned over and hollered into her ear. "Isn't that our captain?"

"Where?" Brooke craned her neck around the dance floor, and Judson shook his head.

"Not down here, up there," he said, pointing with the neck of his beer. She was afraid to look, but there, he was right: behind that pair of mirrored aviators, his hair fabulously disheveled, Saint sat at the drum set, in his own world. *He's a musician, too? Of course he is.* Sweat had dampened his hair, making it seem a darker shade of blond. His black T-shirt seemed painted onto his well-toned chest. In fact, everything about the man seemed darker in this venue, more intense . . . especially when he spotted her. Cool as anything, he slid his sunglasses down his nose and winked. *Why, why, why? Why couldn't he be repulsive? Or better yet, assigned to something else, like commanding troops overseas?*

She gave him a reproving look until Judson's hand waved in front of her face.

"Hey! Space cadet! Do you want another?"

She shook her head; she was concerned enough about her self-control seeing the captain out of a work context. She needed her wits. This was *not good*. Places like this already put her on edge. The smell of greasy food and alcohol, the bass-heavy music, the dark walnut paneling, even the magicked sconces that changed color: it all reminded her of the night she'd met Charlie, Olly's dad. Her guard was up before she'd even sat down in the booth. Judson was still waiting at the bar (he suffered from invisible customer syndrome, politely waiting until everyone else had come and gone before finally being noticed) when Saint's band finished their set.

He's coming over. He's coming over, and I'm alone. She tried to send Judson a desperate mental SOS, but her friend was engaged in some intense flirting with a heavily tattooed woman wearing a shirt that showed her flat midriff. *I looked like that before I gave birth. Enjoy it while you can, girl.*

"Hello, Ms. Everleigh. I didn't know you came here."

"I don't, usually. I mean, I'm not a big club . . . person. Judson wanted to see your band, and as you might expect, he doesn't like to go out by himself. I don't think many people do. We didn't know it was your band, of course, we weren't following you or anything, just a coincidence. An unfortunate one, obviously."

He smirked. "A Brooke who babbles. You're aptly named."

Their lead singer, a large black man with thick dreads, appeared next to him. "Who's your friend?" His face showed that it was more than polite interest that had brought him over.

"We're enemies, actually. This is Brooke; she's a reporter."

"*That* Brooke?"

Saint nodded, and the other man offered his hand. "Tremain. Any enemy of Saint's is a friend of mine."

She gave him a firm, unflirty handshake. "Fair enough. I can always use another friend."

He gestured to her, and hiding her surprise, she slid over so he could sit next to her in the booth. That's when she noticed his hair.

"What's that in your hair, is that . . . a pop top from a can?"

The man grinned, leaning down so she could get a better look. His dreads were full of hardware: nuts, springs, washers, metal beads, paperclips, you name it. She'd seen plenty of dreads before: being the royal standard made them popular for people of all ethnicities, but this was a whole new twist on it.

"Do you take it out when you sleep?"

Tremain sipped his drink—water, from the look of it. "Nope. Always slept on my stomach anyway."

"My mother thinks that's how you get cancer."

Both men laughed; she hadn't noticed that Saint had slid in across from her until just then. Judson came back, standing awkwardly at a distance, before trying to slide away.

"Judd, sit down. He'll scoot over. Scoot over, Captain."

Saint stood up. "Did I take your seat? Apologies." *Interesting; he didn't just yield his seat to Judd. He made him slide over. He's still on the outside, in the dominant position.* Judson slid to the inside seat looking distinctly unhappy that his "girls' night" had been crashed and Brooke smirked at him.

"Brooke's got a little boy, Olly," said Saint.

Why would he say that? Is he trying to scare him off me?

Tremain turned more toward her. "Really? I've got a son, too. How old?"

Oh. No, he was giving common ground. That was . . . nice. "Five."

"Mine's just three last week."

"Oh, congrats. Three's a fun age."

"If you like tantrums, sure."

"Well," Brooke drawled, "being in a band with Captain Saint, I'm sure you've dealt with tantrums before."

Judson and Tremain laughed. Saint glared. Judson stopped suddenly, finding the graffiti on the wall very interesting.

"You're married, then?" Brooke asked, but Tremain shook his head.

"Just found out about the little champ a year ago. His mum didn't tell me."

Brooke nodded slowly. "I didn't tell Olly's dad, either. He caught us together at the library about two months ago, put it together himself. Only one-night stand I ever had." She gave Saint a pointed look. "Just think, Captain, you could have progeny out there, running around."

Saint laughed. "When ships weigh less than chips. I'm very careful."

"So was I," Tremain said ruefully, and an expression flickered across Saint's face that Brooke couldn't quite read. *Doubt?*

"Whereas I have no need for care, as I haven't done the act in ages," Judson said cheerfully, and Brooke reached out and squeezed his hand sympathetically.

"No go with the tattoo girl?"

"Her birthday's on the thirteenth. I can't risk it."

The two musicians looked at him blankly and Brooke hid a smile. "Judson's very superstitious. Fanatically superstitious."

"And rightfully so. There was construction at hospital, so I was born under a ladder. Put me at a disadvantage from my first moment on this earth." No one laughed. "That was a joke."

Brooke smiled at him. In her peripheral vision, she noticed that Saint was looking at her hand, still on Judson's.

"So, you two are together?"

Why does he care?

"Oh, no, we're not together," Brooke said quickly, withdrawing her hand. "Well, we are together in the sense that we came together, but we're not *together* together. We're not seeing each other. We're just friends."

An awkward silence fell over the table. Brooke felt her gaze drawn back to Tremain. He stood, smiling, and Saint followed him. "It was nice to meet you, Brooke. And you . . . ?"

"Judson Boote," he replied. "Loved your set."

"Thanks, man. Good luck getting laid," Tremain called as they headed for the bar.

Judson's face brightened. "Thanks!" Then he sighed. "If only there was such a thing."

"What do you want, a lucky penny or something? A rabbit's foot to rub?"

"If not, I'll be resigned to rub other things."

Brooke threw a peanut at him, and he ducked, squawking. She pulled out her phone. No texts from her mom.

"Put that thing away. Olly's fine."

"You don't know that," she replied, lifting her voice to be heard over the canned music. "Someday, you'll understand."

"I already do understand. You're a control freak who doesn't know how to have fun."

"Having fun is how I'm now a mother." She tried not to stare at Saint, who was talking with a curvy brunette at the bar. Fortunately, his back was to her. Unfortunately, Judson's wasn't.

"Oh, Woz. You have a thing for him."

"Who?"

"Who?" he mimicked her, pitching his voice higher. "You know who: Captain Drum Set. He makes your heart go pitter-patter. Tappity-tap-tap."

She kicked him under the table and he howled. "Number one: I don't. Number two: even if I did, I don't date anymore. And number three: I wouldn't want you broadcasting it to the whole bar if I did—which I don't—now would I?"

"Brooke," he said, leaning forward across the table, "why would it be so bad if you did? I know you're not a trusting soul, but it wouldn't hurt to go easy on the man. He doesn't seem like a bad egg. He's doing you a favor, you know?"

"I just don't see how a nice person can be associated with someone like Edward." Her gaze wandered back to Saint again. "They're good friends, aren't they? If he's so nice, how can he defend someone who's committed such a terrible crime?"

"Maybe he didn't know anything about it," Judson said, sipping his beer. "I could be a cat burglar. You'd never know."

"You're not light enough of foot," she deadpanned, and he grinned.

"What's happening with the story?"

She snorted. "Waiting. We ran the initial story, but until I get some kind of official response beyond 'no comment,' we can't do much else. I'm trying to gather more evidence, but it's slow going. I've got to have a denial or a confirmation, or I've got nothing." She spun her glass, frustrated. "How can I get them to admit it?"

"Are you sure he did it?"

"Don't start again, Judd."

"I just meant that all the evidence hinges on her story . . ."

"Yes!" Brooke slammed her open palm onto the table, drawing attention from nearby drinkers. "But that doesn't make it invalid. What kind of evidence do you want? Do you think they had a magical examiner at the front?"

"Lower your voice. I'm just saying. It's his word against hers."

"But that doesn't mean she's lying!"

"Not saying it does. Just saying that the burden of proof is greater."

"Should we need proof? Why can't we just accept her word?" It went against every journalistic principle she'd ever had, but this went deeper than a normal story. It was a heinous violation of the worst kind, and she was sick of hearing these stories. It had to stop.

"Yes, love. We absolutely need proof. Because otherwise, it would open up magic users everywhere to baseless accusation. You know that wouldn't work. Not everyone is as noble as you."

"Don't tease. I'm serious."

"I'm actually serious as well. You want to ascribe good motivations to everyone because you have good motivations. But there are reasons why a 'victim' might accuse someone apart from actual experience, despite the damage to her reputation. There have always been people willing to set themselves on fire to watch someone else burn."

Brooke leaned forward. "What if it was your mother? Or your sister? Or me? Wouldn't you want someone to believe me, someone to care enough to find out the facts? To press for justice? Even in the face of impossible odds, wouldn't you want someone to try to do the right thing?"

He softened. "Of course I would. But I also don't want to see you made a fool. This is a big step for you. I'd hate to see you get knocked down."

"I'll take the risk."

He lifted his beer bottle to her. "Brooke Amanda Everleigh, defender of victims everywhere. I should get you a cape."

She clinked his bottle with her glass. "I'll take it, in red."

CHAPTER TEN

SAINT SIPPED HIS PALE ale. "Heidi, huh? That's a nice name."

The woman giggled and tossed her dark hair. "Thank you, Captain."

"Please, all my friends call me Saint."

Her smile was coy. "Are we friends, Captain?"

"I think we could be." He grinned. "*Good* friends."

"Mmm, the best kind," she purred.

"Maybe."

It was effortless. It had always been easy, getting women into his bed. But since he'd come back from Op'Ho'Lonia a hero, there was no friction to it at all. Well, except the good kind . . . but it took no convincing. Really, where was the challenge? *If I want a challenge,* he thought as he looked into her mahogany eyes, *I'll challenge Sam to Scrabble or James to Trivial Pursuit. There's no reason this has to be a game.*

Ms. Everleigh laughed behind him, and her words rang in his head . . . *Just think, you could have progeny out there.* Why had he assumed that a woman would tell him if she'd gotten pregnant? Really, he didn't know much about them, nor they about him . . . maybe not even his phone number. It was possible a woman would've concealed it or not known how to contact him, and the thought bothered him.

"Hello? Saint?" Heidi was watching him, her brows drawn together in concern.

He stroked the back of her hand, resting on the bar top. "Sorry. I have a lot on my mind tonight." He smiled: the heated smile James said melted women's pants right off. "I'll be more attentive."

Leaning into him so he could see down her shirt, she whispered into his ear. "I think I could take your mind off your troubles."

"I'd let you try, if you wanted . . ."

"How generous of you."

"I'm a generous guy."

"I'm counting on it," she said, sliding off her barstool. Heidi took his hand and wove between the tables and the couples intertwined on the dance floor. "My place or yours?"

"Yours, beautiful." The answer rolled out of his mouth as he caught sight of Everleigh checking her phone again. *I'd bet my TV she's thinking about Oliver.* Meanwhile, he was getting tugged out of the building by a woman whose name he barely remembered. *Hannah? No, Heidi.* A woman he might impregnate tonight, even if it was by accident.

Another little kid, running around without a dad, just like he had. Another kid like Olly, whose mother would bear the burden of raising him alone, unable to relax on a Saturday night because she was constantly thinking about him. He never wanted to put a woman in that position.

"Wait, Heidi."

She pivoted on the sidewalk, turning a dazzling smile on him.

"I'm sorry. I'm not feeling up to this tonight."

She leaned in for a sultry kiss, her hands sliding over his chest. "Really?"

His body began to argue with him, citing her perfume (nice, not too heavy), her hair (silky, long), and her chest (its comments about this were too explicit to be shared). Maybe he could just make her happy and leave . . . Was that offensive? Would that hurt her feelings? He certainly didn't want her to think it was her; it wasn't. It was 100 percent Everleigh's fault for planting these thoughts, these doubts in his head. *It's not enough that she screws up my life at work? Now she's going after my personal life, too?*

Sighing, he reached up and encircled her wrists, gently pulling them away from his body.

"I'm sorry, I really am. I think I'm coming down with something. I don't want to make you ill."

She pursed her painted lips, a light scowl on her face. He tucked her arm into his.

"Let me walk you back to the bar. I'm sure a beautiful woman like you can find someone else to entertain you tonight . . ."

"I wanted *you* to entertain me."

"Another time, perhaps."

She opened her mouth to argue, when his phone rang. *Saved by the technology.* "Sorry, I've got to take this, it's . . ." He stifled a groan. "It's my gestator."

Heidi blinked. "Your what?" He held up a finger to signal "just a minute."

"Hi, Calynda."

"Baby." She was crying. "Can you come pick me up?"

"What's wrong?"

"Gary took the money you gave me and took off. I don't have a key to get into our apartment, and the manager said he can't let me in unless I'm on the lease. I don't have anywhere to go tonight." There was a tremor in her voice, but he was pretty sure it was panic and not withdrawal.

Saint bit back his "I told you so" and kicked the sidewalk unconsciously. "Where are you?"

"112th and Market."

That's a shitty neighborhood. She can't stand there alone. "Okay. Hang on, I'll be there in a few minutes."

He hung up and leaned over, putting his hands on his knees for support. Being upside down helped. His head might as well match his world at the moment.

"Did you call her your . . . gestator?" Heidi's tone was thick with judgment.

"Yes. As in, the person who gestated me. She didn't mother me in any sense of the word. I've gotta go, love. Let's get you back to the bar." He caught her arm and led her back toward the Rusty Nail until she gently pulled away from him.

"That's okay. I think I'll . . . go home."

"Can I call you a ride?"

"No, I'm good. You go."

He nodded, then gave her a lingering kiss on her made-up cheek. "Sorry."

CALYNDA WAS SHIVERING, coatless in the late Tenth Month chill. "Baby, thank you, thank you for—"

He held up a hand to silence her. He was too tired for her fawning. He tucked his coat around her shoulders and led her back to the train station.

"Are we going to your house?" she asked, the hope painfully obvious in her voice.

"No. I'll get you a hotel room for tonight, and we'll get you back into your old apartment tomorrow."

"What? Why?" She leaned closer to him. "I've been dying to see your new house."

"Not tonight."

"But why?"

Saint gritted his teeth. He didn't want to tell her the truth, that he didn't want the space polluted by her. That she was toxic, and he wanted his home untouched by her.

"Not tonight."

"But baby . . ."

"Stop calling me that, Calynda. You can't come to my house. You haven't earned that privilege yet."

Her eyes filled with tears, but she said nothing until they said their goodbyes at the door of room 104 of the Sleep-the-Night-Away Hotel. Saint's last thought before he exited the building was that most of the people he'd passed didn't look like they'd be doing much sleeping that night, and he wasn't sure if he envied them or not.

CHAPTER ELEVEN

TWO DAYS LATER, SAINT got a text.

Brooke: I am going to drop Oliver at your house on Wednesday.

Brooke: What time shall I come?

Saint: You've decided to trust me? I'm honored.

Brooke: What. time. you. smooth-brained. imbecile?

Saint: 5:15. You were thirty minutes late last time, so that should get you here by 5:45.

That pissed her off, he thought, chuckling, as the dots pulsed on the screen longer than usual. *Just because she's being insulting doesn't mean I have to be. I should take the high road.* His mum would definitely not approve of how he'd treated her so far.

Brooke: I'll be there at 5:45, Captain.

Saint: Have him bring a coat.

SAINT'S DOORBELL RANG at 5:56. *Well, only eleven minutes late this time. That's an improvement over thirty . . .* He opened the door. Oliver was in tears, and Brooke was pink-cheeked and furious. She looked more frustrated than a surgeon without a scalpel.

"Hello, Captain. I apologize for our tardiness. I'll be back at seven to get him."

"You said he could come to our house. You promised," Oliver sniffled.

"For the king's sake, Oll . . ." Brooke sighed, then turned to Saint. "Sorry. Thanks."

Saint's phone flashed to life, and he tipped it up to see who it was. *Calynda Huxley.* He rejected the call. "All right, Private Oliver. Stand at attention."

He hesitated a moment, then threw his small shoulders back, and his head snapped up to meet Saint's gaze.

"Good. About face."

"That means turn around," Brooke whispered, and he did. Saint put his hands on his charge's shoulders. "Forward march."

"Where are you taking him?" Brooke's tone was defensive again, and Saint sighed. Someone had done a number on this woman's trust; what wasn't his fault was quickly becoming his problem. He spoke slowly, enunciating every word.

"We are going to play basketball at my gym. It is just down the street. It has a café, where we will eat when we are done."

She dug in her purse and came up with a twenty-dollar bill. "There you go."

He ignored her outstretched hand, but softened his tone slightly. "The program gives me a stipend for activities."

"I insist. We don't need charity."

Based on what I've seen? You definitely do. "I'm not allowed to accept gifts. Didn't you read the instructions?"

He started Olly down the sidewalk again, and Brooke followed.

"Yes, I did read the instructions. It didn't say anything about not taking money for food for my kid. It said that you couldn't accept gifts *in order to curry favor*. Since I have zero interest in your favor, I see no discrepancy."

"Fine. Whatever." He took the money and shoved it in his front jeans pocket. "See you later, Mum."

"Text me the address, and I'll pick him up there." She was turning to go back to the train, and they paused at the intersection. "Goodbye, love," she said, ruffling Olly's hair. He turned his face away, crossing his arms over his belly halfheartedly. She was obviously uncomfortable leaving him, and Saint didn't know if it was his fault or Olly's.

Leave already. He'll be fine. He forced himself to slow his breathing, knowing that his tension would just add to hers.

"Say goodbye to your mum, Oliver."

"Bye." His voice was dry ice, painful.

Watching the resignation and humiliation on her face, Saint felt an inkling of empathy for her, just an internal pinch of emotion. She wasn't a bad mum; he'd seen some of those. Mums who couldn't draw boundaries or put their foot down. That wasn't Everleigh. She turned and walked quickly down the sidewalk, swiping at her face, which he guessed was now stained with tears.

With a sigh, Saint got Oliver moving again toward the gym.

"What was that all about, mate?"

"She broke her promise. It's not fair." He wiped his running nose on his coat sleeve. At least she'd remembered to send him with a jacket. "She said you could come to our house. Now she went to Grandma's without me."

"Sounds pretty disappointing." *Teach your mentee to identify their own emotions with a healthy dose of empathy: there is power in naming something, in being understood.* He had the manual memorized by now.

"What's that?"

"Disappointing? When it's not what you wanted or expected to happen."

"Yes. It's dizabointing."

Saint bit the inside of his cheek so he wouldn't smile, nodding his head. "I get it. I was hoping your mum would stay, too."

"You were?" Olly seemed surprised. "She said you don't like her because she tells the truth."

That erased all his empathy. "Did she say why she had to change our plans?"

"Yes. Gran's moving away. We're not going to see her anymore. Mum has to help." *Yikes. Another babysitter gone for a single mum . . .*

"Oh, that's sad. But it sounds like Gran really needed her help, eh? You and I can hang out together for a bit while she takes care of that. You'd have likely been bored if she took you with her."

Olly let out a thin sigh. "I guess." He hurried to match Saint's longer stride. "Does the café have burgers?"

"You know it." He held up his hand for a high five, and Olly jumped for it. Then Saint reached into his pocket to retrieve her twenty dollars. "Give this back to your mum for me, will you, mate? Thanks."

CHAPTER TWELVE

BROOKE HURRIED DOWN the sidewalk in her black skirt suit on Friday. She was nearly to the courthouse, but her high heels weren't cooperating. The polygraph was set to start in ten minutes, and she wasn't even in the building yet. She checked her watch again, willing time to *please slow down* and pulled at her coat to wrap her neck more tightly. It was definitely turning colder. Her pea coat needed to last her at least one more year . . . It had been missing a button when she pulled it out of storage (dumb mice), but she'd sewn on another one that was close enough. It was the right size and color, but it had four holes instead of two. *You'd never notice if you didn't look closely,* she told herself. It was still going to bother her.

When she found the room, the security guard was just closing the door.

"Wait, wait, wait!" she whispered loudly, and the black man paused, then smiled as she squeezed by him inside. Brooke collapsed into the only available chair, front row center.

"Knew you'd be late," Saint whispered. A woman sitting on his other side, dressed entirely in black with long black hair, raised an eyebrow at them both.

Brooke said nothing, her chest still heaving. She was afraid her voice would be too loud in the quiet room if she tried to bicker with him now. She'd come up with something good and zing him later. *When you least expect it, Captain Sinner. Like a Taser in a dark alley.* She glanced around, nodding to reporters from a few other outlets, who nodded back. She didn't know who the rest of the people in the room were . . . interested observers, perhaps? More palace staff? Saint was the only one in uniform. It looked good on him. *Of course it does.*

"Good morning, we're going to get started now." The tan-skinned man put a hand on his chest. "I'm Silas Greene, and I'll be administering the test today. This is Mrs. Greta Burnham, and I'll be asking her some questions regarding the incident that allegedly took place last year. The first few questions will be to establish a baseline response."

A thought occurred to Brooke, and she leaned over to Saint. "Did you save this seat for me?"

He nodded, then whispered back. "It's easier to gloat if you're right next to me."

Donkey.

Greta sat in the chair, and a blue bubble formed around it, wavering slowly, wobbling, a delicate spherical stream moving around her. It was a little unnerving; Brooke wasn't used to being able to see the magic that surrounded them and made their electronics possible. Unlike Veil Technicians, she couldn't see or feel it, ever. Some people were gifted with a natural ability to form a relationship with the magic; receptiveness, an innate capability. Since it was lucrative work, she probably should've tried to develop one anyway, but it wasn't really that interesting to her. Science wasn't her thing.

Brooke opened her phone and hit record.

"Is your name Greta Patricia Burnham?" Mr. Greene asked.

"Yes." The bubble vibrated silently, then turned green, before fading slowly back to blue.

"Are you twenty-three years old?"

"Yes."

Geez, really? She looks a lot older. It was her makeup, Brooke decided. She wasn't doing something right around her eyes. *Winged her eyeliner too much, maybe? It isn't doing her any favors.*

"Are you from Attaamy?"

"Yes." *Green.* Greta swiped at her mouth with a white handkerchief. She looked outwardly very calm and collected in her ash-gray suit and emerald-green blouse.

"Were you at the front near Tupelo Crossing on the twenty-first of Fourth Month?"

"Yes." *Green.*

"Did you see King Edward on that day?"

"Yes." *Green.*

"Did he kiss you?"

She paused, and Brooke could see tears dancing in her eyes.

"Mrs. Burnham, answer the question, please."

"Yes," she whispered. *Green.* The woman in black next to Saint leaned over and whispered something to him, and he nodded.

"Did you tell anyone that day?"

"No." *Green.*

"Did you tell someone later?"

"Yes." *Green.*

"Did His Majesty ask you to turn a blind eye?"

Brooke looked around; she'd never heard that expression before. *What does that mean?*

"Yes." *Green.*

"I'm sorry to interrupt." Saint's deep voice startled her. "But I'm not familiar with that expression. Could you please explain it?"

"Certainly, Captain," Mr. Green said. "It means 'Did he ask you to disregard what had happened?'"

"Thank you."

Brooke noticed a lot of people scribbling down notes. Clearly, she wasn't the only one who didn't know what it meant.

"Two more questions, Mrs. Burnham, and then we'll be done." Mr. Greene cleared his throat. "Do you live on Howard Street?"

"No." *Green.*

"Did His Majesty try to contact you after the incident?"

"No." *Green.*

"Thank you, Mrs. Burnham." Greta stood, the bubble dissolving around her, tears silently streaming down her face, and Brooke wished she could give the poor woman a hug. Mrs. Burnham shook Mr. Greene's hand, and then her lawyer and her husband were quickly whisking her from the conference room.

Brooke stopped her phone recording, then cocked her head, listening. "That's a sweet sound."

"What is?" Saint asked, his arms folded across his chest.

"The sound of no one gloating." She smiled, then turned on her high heels and walked out of the conference room without looking back.

BROOKE LAY AWAKE IN bed that night. It was that one question that nagged at her still: turn a blind eye? Everyone else was confused by the administrator's turn of phrase, but not Mrs. Burnham; she'd answered immediately. She'd known exactly what he meant. Brooke had already done an internet search for the phrase and found that it was a common phrase in Attaamy. But the polygraph administrator wouldn't be likely to know that . . . and he wouldn't be likely to know that Mrs. Burnham wasn't from Orangiers; her accent was so light, Brooke would guess that most people missed it. Brooke turned on her computer and typed in the administrator's name to do a background check. Her initial search produced junky results . . . others who were clearly too old or too young.

She drummed her fingers on her desk, yawning. *Why can't I be the kind of person who just lets things go?* Brooke felt herself taking the first steps of a journey that could take the rest of the night once she started the deep dive into the nooks and crannies of the subject . . . She read about polygraph tests. She read about the extensive training in magic that test administrators had to undergo. She read about infamous people who'd cheated the test—they'd used a false baseline by causing themselves pain when the true questions were asked, so that their variation seemed less noticeable between the truth and the lies. One cheater had used thumb tacks, another bit their tongue. *The handkerchief.* Why else would she wipe her mouth like that? Had she drawn blood?

She read about Greta, what little she could find online. Perhaps there would be more in the library archives. She switched over to the online database and went through page after page . . . Her mind drifted back to the time she'd looked up Saint's mother, and she wondered . . .

Brooke had gained access into Attaamy's public records for a story last year. What were the odds her login still worked? Of course there wasn't a background check for Greta in Orangiers, but there might be a better one in Attaamy.

GRETA PATRICIA BURNHAM

Born on the fourth day of Third Month in the year 495 to Florence and Tegaard Barnswallow. One brother, Drake Silas Barnswallow. Deceased.

Married to Ralph J. Burnham in the year 515.

Silas. That was it: it had to be. Mr. Greene, or whoever he was, was her brother. And if they were related, he could've been building up a secondary relationship with the magic on her behalf; by basically thinking about her in the presence of the magic, he convinced it that she was friendly and allowed his casting to fall over her as well. They'd cheated.

That's why they both knew the expression; they were from the same place. Despite the early hour, Brooke took out her phone and dialed Mrs. Burnham's number. It went immediately to voicemail.

"Hi Greta, it's Brooke Everleigh. Please call me when you get this; I need to meet with you, it's urgent."

She would wait to be angry. She would wait until she talked to her first. She would give her the benefit of the doubt for a few more hours . . . and then, she would release her wrath.

CHAPTER THIRTEEN

BROOKE WAS WAITING at the same café they'd met at originally, knee bouncing under the table, mug of tea empty already. Greta arrived with her husband, and her steps sped up as she caught Brooke's fake joyful expression.

"Greta! You did it, this is exactly the proof we needed to move forward. I'm so happy for you. Your article is going to be published tomorrow, as soon as I finish the write-up. Congratulations." She shook the woman's hand and didn't miss her knowing glance at her husband. "I just have a few more questions for you. Will you sit?"

"Certainly," she said, smiling demurely. "What's on your mind?"

"I realize this might be painful, but in my research, I came across an article about your brother. It mentioned that he had died . . . Could you expand on the circumstances of his death?"

She nodded soberly, but her husband put a hand on her elbow, his gaze sharpening.

"What does this have to do with the incident?" Ralph asked.

"Oh, it's just part of the background. They wanted a wider profile."

Greta piped up. "It's okay, lovebug. He was lost at sea, sadly, as a young man."

"Oh, how tragic. And they never found the body?"

"I'm afraid not, no."

"He's not living in Orangiers under an assumed identity, then?"

Mrs. Burnham waited a beat too long to answer, her eyes bouncing around Brooke's face, trying to read her, before she let out a quiet laugh. "Of course not."

Brooke pulled out the photograph she'd found of him on social media. "That's funny, because he looks exactly like Mr. Greene."

"Woz-condemn-it," Greta seethed. "You are not going to ruin this for me. I've worked too hard, put too much on the line to—"

Brooke pointed a finger at her. "You lied to me." She stood calmly to make her escape as the couple stared at her, open-mouthed. "And even worse, you have spit on the struggle of people who have legitimately been injured by magic users like this. You'll be hearing from the newspaper's lawyer."

"He should never have been made king!" Greta screamed after her. "This is Edward's own fault for marrying that matriarchal witch—Lincoln and Heather were born to rule, not waste away in exile!"

Brooke walked faster, trying to get out onto the street, where there would be more onlookers in case they tried something violent. Maybe she should've brought someone with her, but she'd hoped so dearly that she'd been wrong. She rushed to meet the train that was just pulling in, and when she got back to work she walked straight into Miranda's office.

"We have to kill the Greta Burnham story."

Her editor turned her chair around, and Brooke saw that she was on the phone. She motioned for Brooke to sit, and Brooke closed the door before she complied.

"Uh-huh. Yes, of course." She listened for another moment before interjecting. "Love, someone's just walked in, I've got to go." She listened, massaging her temple with her free hand. "Yes. We'll do that. I've got to go now. Talk to you soon." She hung up. "Spill it."

"They made the whole thing up. Story's dead. Polygraph administrator is her brother, he helped her cheat. They must've had someone else bend her mind and steal that ring. If I figured it out, someone else will, too. I'm sure Captain Saint is just behind me."

"In more ways than you know."

There was a knock at the door. "Come in," Miranda called.

Captain Saint entered. *Of course.* He shut the door behind him and sat down next to Brooke without being invited.

"Made yourself comfortable?"

"Not by half." He grinned, and Brooke rolled her eyes, pursing her lips to keep a smile off them. He sobered then, handing a thumb drive to Miranda. "Here's the evidence we discussed."

Miranda took the thumb drive and put it in her computer, which blinked to life. She motioned to Brooke to join her behind the desk. As she passed Saint, she pinched the back of his right arm and he jumped, glaring.

Brooke leaned over to see the screen better, and Saint cleared his throat, staring pointedly at her chest; her neckline had dropped to reveal her cleavage, and she hauled it back up and held it with one hand, glaring at him.

"What am I looking at?" Miranda asked, her voice even as ever.

"This is security footage from the airfield in Imahara, when Edward left the front to escort Abelia across Gratha. The time and date are in the corner." On the screen, a tall black man with a regal bearing walked across the terminal, and someone ran up to him and handed him a slip of paper he'd dropped. When he turned, they could see it was Edward's face.

"Left the front?" Brooke felt faint. "That was never . . ."

"Never publicized? No. Most of our own troops didn't even know that he'd gone. You can understand why we didn't want this spread around, I'm sure. We're only sharing it now to put this story to rest for good. It seemed necessary after the polygraph test yesterday." His face showed no anxiety. Brooke wondered how he hid it so well. He could've showed her this weeks ago . . . but that would require something they hadn't had then. Trust.

Saint was taking a chance, showing it to them now. He must be more desperate than she'd realized. Crossing back to her seat, Brooke reached into her bag and pulled out a manila envelope.

"Here." She offered it to Saint, who hesitantly took it.

"What's this?"

"Everything you need to prosecute Silas Greene and Greta and Ralph Burnham for slander and conspiracy." She turned to Miranda. "Don't worry, I've got copies. I'm going to go to home and write up the whole thing. I'll have it on your desk by the morning."

"Wait." Saint's eyebrows were a deep V. "You can't—"

"Don't worry. I'll keep the video out of it. I've got plenty of evidence without it." She paused. "Please tell the king I'm sorry." Brooke walked out, unable to look at their faces for fear of reading pity or scorn on them. Both possibilities were equally horrible.

She felt numb as she walked out of the offices. Several people congratulated her on her article, shook her hand. She didn't correct them. They'd find out soon enough.

Everyone would. Everyone would know how wrong she'd been. Everyone would see how she'd tried to destroy the king's reputation, damage his image. Her boots felt filled with cement as she walked down the road, her shoulders bowed with a weight none could see. Not only had Greta used her, but that woman's actions would now be used to prove why people shouldn't listen to other people when they claimed they'd been mistreated or abused. And that pissed her off more than any damage to her career ever could. She'd given them a talking point that would hurt victims for years to come.

Rather than writing, Brooke went home and worked out with a video, throwing all her weight into the cross-punches and nearly pulling a muscle on the roundhouse kicks. It helped a little. Then she wrote until it was time to go get Olly and tucked her laptop into her bag. She'd packed them a picnic dinner, and they could play and eat at the park until bedtime.

She might as well make Olly happy today; she'd failed with everyone else.

CHAPTER FOURTEEN

SAINT HAD JUST CRACKED open a celebratory beer when there was a faint, unsteady knock at his door. Buster lifted his head but didn't bark. Saint paused his show and jogged over to the door, expecting James; he'd texted that he was coming over with birthday/victory cake. Saint was more than ready to relax after the week's troubling events . . . He'd taken a chance, showing Brooke and her editor that video. She'd taken a bigger one, putting that evidence in his hands, especially after she'd just taken such a huge hit. It was too confusing to think about right now.

But rather than his friend's face, it was Brooke's wide blue eyes that met him when he opened the door.

"Hello, Captain," said Oliver.

"Hello, Olly. What are you doing out past bedtime, mate?"

"Someone played in our apartment and made an awful mess while Mummy was out."

Saint's eyes snapped to Brooke's and she gave a slight nod.

"Oh, that's awful, mate. Come in, Everleighs, come in and take your shoes off. Are you hungry?" She just stared at him, like a statue someone had plunked down in front of his door.

"I could eat," Olly replied and tromped inside, plopping himself down on the couch. He laughed as Buster went nuts, licking his face, his tail knocking everything off the coffee table. "Can I watch the telly?"

"It's not for kids, mate—let me find you something better . . ." He grabbed his dog by the collar to get his attention, then snapped and pointed to his bed, and Buster slunk off to go lie down. "Brooke, come in." His hand on her elbow revealed why she hadn't come inside; she was trembling so badly, he didn't know how she was still standing. He tucked her under his arm and led her inside, supporting her. His instinct was to pick her up and carry her, but he didn't know how to explain that to Olly, who seemed to be largely untroubled by the evening's events so far. Saint managed to get her to the kitchen table and into a chair. He rummaged around to find something edible for Olly. He held up a half-eaten bag of crisps he'd swiped from Bluffton, and she nodded faintly.

Telly on kid stuff, Olly with the crisps, he knelt in front of Brooke.

"Your place got broken into?"

She nodded.

"Are you hurt?"

She shook her head.

"You're frightening me with your silent routine, Babbling Brooke . . ." He let his hand rest on her knee, and she started to cry. *Shit.*

"Where's your phone, love?"

She patted her pockets until she found it and handed it to him.

"You've not called your mum or the police . . . Would you like to do that now?"

She shook her head vehemently, and her tears came faster.

"Okay." He held up his hands in surrender, setting her phone on the table. "Okay, bad idea." Saint tried to think. *Maybe I should call my mum to come over or at least advise me on the situation. She would probably not be thrilled about the idea of an unmarried woman sleeping in my house . . . She might insist they go to hers. But Olly would probably be more comfortable here.* He did some inside-his-head cursing for a minute, then sighed.

Brooke was still crying, watching him. "They wrote things on the door," she whispered. "Bad things. I didn't want Olly to see."

He got her a tissue and handed it to her, then knelt in front of her again. "You'll stay here tonight, won't you? Please?" A tiny smirk appeared at the corner of her mouth, and he grinned. "Oh, she thinks I'm begging. Very funny, woman. Don't let my posture fool you; I have my pride."

"I'm sorry for crashing—" she started, but he cut her off.

"Don't. Don't apologize, please. This isn't your fault." He put his hands on her knees and looked into her eyes. "Everleigh, this is not your fault, all right? Not Burnham, not Lincoln's rabid supporters. None of this."

"Right," she murmured, and her gaze went soft. "Thank you." She brought up her hands to cover both of his, and he felt his heart begin to pound. It would be easy, so easy, to pull her forward and meet her lips with his own . . .

When did I start thinking of her like that? Hastily, he pulled back, getting to his feet.

"I'll just go change the sheets. You two will have the bed, I'll crash on the couch."

"No, don't go to any trouble . . ."

"Everleigh, this isn't a discussion. Your sense of safety was violated tonight. You'll get better rest in the bed. Woz knows I've slept on the couch a time or two anyway. It'll be just fine for a few nights."

"My mum's out of town, should be back day after tomorrow. We'll be out of your hair then."

"You're not in my hair now." *In my chest, maybe, mucking about. But not in my hair.*

He passed through the living room to find Olly asleep on the floor in front of the flashing TV, his hand still in the bag of crisps, and Saint chuckled. The smaller a person was, the more prone to ridiculous behavior they were, he thought to himself. Of course, there were outliers like James. And Abbie. But still.

Saint texted James not to come, then changed the sheets to the white set and pulled down extra blankets in case they were cold in the night, then a sleeping bag for himself. Realizing the bedroom was kind of a mess, he snatched up the boxer shorts and dirty workout shirts off the floor and stuffed them into the hamper. *Is there anything in here a kid shouldn't see?* Glancing toward the empty doorway, he got down on all fours to try to see at "kid level," in case there was something he'd missed. Saint looked over to see Brooke's ankles. He looked up.

"This isn't what it looks like."

"Sure it is," she said. "You're checking to make sure it's safe for Olly."

He sat back on his heels. "Right. It's exactly what it looks like, then." His memory triggered at the word *safe*, and he got to his feet. He pulled out the hunting knife he kept in the nightstand and tucked it in the top drawer of the dresser, where the boy couldn't reach. "That's better." He pointed to the closed drawer. "Feel free to employ that if anyone startles you in the night."

"Even you?"

"Especially me. Just let me grab my pajamas, and I'll be out of *your* hair . . . Oh, here, there's an extra set of pajama pants for you. They're too long, certainly, but you could roll them . . ." *Oh no. Not the long stare. Control, man.* "And here's a T-shirt. It's clean." Her eyes were pleading with him for comfort. *Stay in control. Her son is in the other room . . . It wouldn't do for him to find Mummy getting naked with Captain Saint.*

Brooke stood in the doorway, massaging her own temples, rubbing her face, and then he saw her shoulders start to shake again.

Oh no. Emotional need. *Oh no.* His defenses were crumbling. *It's just one night. I will hold it together for her. She's falling apart, but she doesn't need me that way.*

He found himself nodding, setting down the clothes on top of the dresser, drawing her into his arms.

"I'm sorry," she sniffled. "I didn't mean to make your life so miserable. I never meant to accuse an innocent man. Everything lined up with her story, she had witnesses . . . I really thought . . ."

"It's okay. I didn't exactly make yours easy, either," he replied.

"Are we declaring a truce?"

"Well, I don't hug my enemies, so I think maybe we should."

He found himself moving his feet, shuffling against the carpet, and she did, too, a slow dance without accompaniment; neither of them minded. He let his cheek rest on the top of her head. He'd never held a woman like this before, giving without asking anything in return.

"Then in the interest of full disclosure, I know all about Calynda."

He stopped moving. "You do?"

She nodded, making no move to let him go. "I do. I saw her name on your phone when you came for pizza. I looked her up. I'm sorry I invaded your privacy. I'm not planning to use the information."

"Wow, I . . . I don't know what to say to that."

Brooke wiped her face with her sleeve. "My dad died when I was very young. And my mother . . . my mother struggled with alcohol after that. I'm sure it's nothing like what you went through, but I understand a little more than some, maybe . . ."

"I'm sorry, Brooke." He squeezed her. "Thanks for keeping it to yourself."

"You're not mad?"

"Why would I be mad? It's your job to dig for a story. I'm the one who left my phone out."

At the feeling of a warm woman in his arms, disclosing her secret loyalty, Saint's body decided to start its launch sequence without authorization from mission control. His instincts told him that she wouldn't turn away . . . but that wasn't why she was here. She'd said no, she'd said never.

And deep inside himself, that wasn't what he wanted, either; not right now, anyway. He found her attractive, of course, but to his own surprise, he was happy just holding her. But he couldn't tell that to his body. Still afraid he might change his mind, he backed away before he could act on his body's many delicious suggestions on what to do with the person pressed against him. "I'll just get Olly," he muttered. "You can change in the bathroom. The door . . . locks."

The door locks? Why not just tell her how dirty your mind is right now? Are you trying to send her running to a hotel? Like she's got money for that.

"If you'd prefer, I can send you to a hotel for tonight . . . my treat."

She shook her head. "I'd feel better with someone else close by."

"Right." Saint headed back down the hall to scoop up Olly, careful not to let his head flop. The kid was heavier than he looked. He eased the boy's prone body sideways through the bedroom door and set him on the bed where he'd pulled back the covers. He tucked him in tight like his dad used to do . . . and suddenly realized that parents do that to try to keep kids in the bed. *My dad's a genius.* Brooke still hadn't changed her clothes; she stood watching him in the doorway with those beautiful eyes. *Speed. Speed, man; put some distance between you.*

"Well, good night, then."

"Saint?"

He turned back.

"It's only 7:30. Are you really going to sleep now?"

"Oh." He chuckled sheepishly, rubbing the back of his neck, looking around. "I guess not. You want a drink or something?" *NO. NO ALCOHOL, do not introduce liquor into this situation, it will not improve things . . .*

She shook her head, turning back toward his bedroom.

"Brooke?"

"Yes?" Her voice was small. She didn't turn.

"Why'd you come here? Why not to Judson, or to your cousin? I don't mind at all that you did, I just . . ." He trailed off.

"I don't know. I just thought Olly'd be comfortable here."

"Right." He cleared his throat. "Okay. Well, good night."

"Good night."

FRANCIS WOKE TO A SMALL face peering at him.

"Woz! Olly. What's wrong, mate?" It had been a bad night of sleep. He knew it was unlikely that the people Brooke had pissed off would follow her here, but every sound, every creak, had had him sitting up all night. He wished he'd kept the knife for himself.

"I'm hungry."

Saint ran a hand over his face. "Right. Okay." He looked around. "Where's your mum?"

"Still in bed. It's your flat; don't you know where the food is?"

Saint scowled. "Yes, sassy britches, I do know where the food is. Come on. Cereal all right?"

He nodded. "I like a blue bowl."

"All I have is white . . ." He looked around for a bargaining chip. "But you can eat it with a serving spoon if you want."

"All right."

Saint poured the shredded-wheat cereal, and Oliver made a face.

"How many bites?"

"Pardon?"

"Sometimes Mummy says I have to eat five bites to get something else. How many bites?"

"Um." Saint poked his head into the fridge. "I could put whipped cream on top?"

Olly nodded. "Did we get robbed?"

Shit. This is a mum conversation, not a mentor conversation. To lie or not to lie? He found the truth always went over best in the communications office . . . Hopefully Brooke would agree. After all, Olly already knew anyway.

"Yes. But it's all right, you're safe here with me."

"Did they take my RC car?"

"I don't know, mate. But if they did, I'll get you a new one. A better one, even."

"Why did they take our stuff?"

"Don't know."

"Who did it?"

He did know, of course; it had to be loyalists supporting absent Lincoln's continued claim. But saying that to the boy would accomplish nothing. So Saint shrugged.

Olly shook his head, disgusted. "Don't you know anything?"

He leaned forward toward the boy, his elbows on the counter, his gaze level. "Well, I know I'm going to have the best Saturday ever now that you're here. What kind of mischief shall we get into?"

CHAPTER FIFTEEN

BROOKE WOKE TO QUIET. Rather than wrapping her in a peaceful calm, it made her instantly nervous. She reached over. The other side of the bed was empty.

"Olly?" she whispered, panicked. "Oh, Olly, don't bother Captain Saint on Saturday morning . . . Olly, where are you, love?" She looked under the bed; she'd found him there many times at home. There was nothing except a pair of boxer shorts and a black guitar case. *I knew he was a boxers man.* Unfortunately for Brooke, her mind collected facts like this and wasn't liable to let this one go anytime soon. Every time he said "briefing," she'd now have to remember looking under his bed and seeing his black-and-white plaid boxers.

Brooke refocused her search. Olly wasn't in the bathroom, nor in the linen closet . . . which was surprisingly tidy. *Military men.*

"Olly?" she whispered again, coming into the living room. Saint's sleeping bag was flopped open, empty. Since Olly didn't seem to be in the flat, at least that bode well for them being together, wherever they were. That's when she saw Buster, sitting at attention, staring intently at the front door. Her son's excited giggles came through the front windows, and she peeked out through the blinds, separating two of the horizontal slats with her fingers. *What on earth?*

Olly had a wooden baseball bat, and Saint was positioning him next to the house.

"You've gotta face away from the house in case you get a good arm on it, you look like you could put it through a window with those muscles." They hadn't seen her yet. Saint backed up and went over to a bucket. Were those . . . water balloons? At this time of year?

Yes, and he was going to pitch them to Olly like a baseball. *Underhand, nice and easy, Captain.* Saint took a step forward and tossed it just like she would've . . . not that she ever would've thought of water balloon baseball in her wildest dreams. Olly swung and missed, and the balloon popped against the house. Both of them laughed maniacally.

"Try again, mate, you'll get the next one. Keep your eye on it." He started to swing his arm back, then stopped. "You know, I've no clue what that means, it's just something my mates used to say."

"What about your dad?"

"My dad preferred basketball, which is funny because he's five foot nothing." Saint shook his head, laughing lightly. He hadn't gelled his hair this morning, and it was adorably tousled.

"I don't have a dad."

"Wish you did?"

Her sweet boy shrugged a shoulder. "Sometimes."

So do I, baby. But not the one life gave you. The little I knew of him, he was so self-absorbed and vain, he'd probably be crap with you. Unlike this guy, apparently.

Saint gestured to the balloons. "Again?"

Olly nodded eagerly. Saint swung his arm back, and this time, Olly caught a piece of it and it exploded against his bat. He stood, arms out like a scarecrow, coat soaked, hair dripping, before they both dissolved into more laughter. Brooke laughed, too, shaking her head at their antics. Something on the kitchen table caught her eye: there was a note.

Brooke—

There's fresh coffee in the pot. Went to the market for better breakfast stuff. My friend Sam is going to come take you to make the police report this afternoon, so I can stay with O.

—Saint

By the look of things, Saint had offered Olly healthy food and been rejected, given the soggy state of the cereal still in the bowl. She opened the fridge. Unlike last night, there was now food in it: donuts (some of which were missing), chocolate milk (open), a bag of salad, a take and bake vegetarian pizza, a loaf of wheat bread, a jar of natural peanut butter, and a jar of jam. *That'll do.* She poured herself some coffee and went back down the hall. If they were having fun—and they seemed to be—who was she to interrupt them?

She curled up in his comfortable flannel sheets, holding the mug with both hands. She knew a long list of things to do was waiting for her—police report; notifying her boss that her files might be missing; cataloguing what had been taken; getting her front door fixed and scrubbing off the nasty red words—but all that could wait a few minutes. Brooke pressed her face into the pillow and smelled Saint's cologne still on it faintly. *Why'd you come here?* Lord only knew. He'd accepted the answer she'd given . . . Too bad it wasn't true.

Because I knew you'd take us in without question. Because you always remember I'm a vegetarian. Because you make my boy laugh and play with him because you want to. Because I told you "never" and you respect that. Because I was so, so wrong, and you didn't rub it in my face.

Because I don't hate you anymore.

AFTER LUNCH, OLLY DECIDED they should all break in the new crayons they'd gotten at the store on their grocery run, and after running around outside, sitting for a while sounded fine to Brooke. Buster was doing his part under the table, chewing up a purple one that had fallen to the ground unnoticed.

Saint reached for the box to replace his black crayon for a brown one and dumped his ice water onto his lap. "Oh shii—take."

Brooke gave him a wide-eyed look, trying not to giggle.

"What's shiitake?" Olly asked, looking up from his drawing.

"Shiitakes? Oh, well, shiitakes, shiitakes are a type of mushroom," he said, pointlessly dabbing at his drenched pants. "Very delicious. I feel very . . . exclamatory. When I think about them."

"Oh. I hate mushrooms." It was true. He routinely picked them off everything, which was sad because she loved them.

"Say 'I don't care for mushrooms,'" Brooke corrected.

"What do you care for?" Saint asked.

"Pizza."

Saint tsked. "Everyone likes pizza. Be an original, Private Everleigh. What else?"

"Mum's buns. She makes them on Christmas."

"I too appreciate your mum's buns," he said, straight-faced.

Brooke leaned back and caught his eye. "Stop it," she mouthed, reddening. Olly might be five, but he wasn't an idiot. He was going to get them in trouble.

Saint smirked, turning back to his drawing. "Mums love it when their sons appreciate their culinary efforts."

"What's culinary?"

"Food-making."

"Did your mum make you cinnamon buns on Christmas?"

"No," he said, "my mum's from Imahara. They don't favor cinnamon buns there."

Brooke looked up in surprise. Saint's face was impassive, but he seemed perfectly serious. *Then again, he always does.*

"Don't tease him, Captain." Calynda was from Orangiers, she was sure of it.

He didn't look up from his battle drawing. "I'm not teasing. My mum and dad are from Imahara. When Calynda went to prison, I was adopted by the Maki family."

"Oh." She searched for something to say, but it was like rattling an empty cookie jar. Another "oh" was the only crumb that fell out.

"What did she make?" Olly asked, filling in his castle with red bricks.

"Fried chicken and strawberry shortcake."

"No!" Brooke laughed. "For Christmas? No roast, no potatoes?"

"Nope." He grinned. "Fried chicken and strawberry shortcake. Every year. I've no idea why."

"How funny."

"You'd like her," he said, glancing up and down in a flash. "She'd like you, too. She has no patience for wicked men."

"I have to pee," Olly announced, getting up from the table.

"Shiitake?" she whispered when the boy was out of range. "Really?"

He held his arms out. "I punted, all right? Like 'sugar' is so much better. You sound like you should have pigtails and a lollipop."

"Does the schoolgirl thing do it for you, Captain?"

He leaned closer to her across Olly's empty chair. "I don't know. You offering to model for me?" His teasing gaze dropped to her lips, and she felt her heartbeat quicken. *Does he want to kiss me? Do I want him to kiss me?* The door opened behind them, and they quickly returned to their respective artwork. Olly came back to the table, wiping his damp hands on his pants.

"Did you use soap?" Brooke asked, sliding back into mum mode.

He nodded, bending his head to continue working on his drawing. "When are we going to meet her, then?"

"Who?" Saint asked, confused.

"Your mum. You said she'd like my mum. So when are we going to meet her?"

His mouth opened, but no sound came out.

Brooke snickered and mockingly put the crayon she was holding to her mouth like a microphone. "Francis Saint, you're the chief communications officer for His Majesty, and you've just been stymied by a five-year-old's simple question. Tell me, in your own words, how does that feel?" She offered him the crayon microphone, and Saint glared at her. Unfazed, she put her chin in her other hand, resting her elbow on the table, staring at him, waiting for an answer.

"Tomorrow, then?" Olly asked, head down, still drawing.

"Soon, mate." Saint stood up. "I'm gonna go change my clothes. I'll be right back."

CHAPTER SIXTEEN

BY THE TIME HE CAME back, Brooke had her coat and shoes on, standing by the front door.

"Where are you going?" The sharpness of his own voice surprised him like a paper cut.

"To my apartment, if you can believe. Olly, you stay here with Captain Saint. Don't watch too much TV."

Despite her dirty shoes, Saint pulled her into the kitchen by her elbow. "You can't go in there yet," he said, trying to drop his voice so the boy wouldn't hear.

"And why is that?"

"There could be a curse on the place, Brooke. You don't know what some of these people are like. These are Lincoln's people; he tried to kill the grand duchess. They won't hesitate to harm you, either."

She watched him quietly for a moment, still not looking convinced, then sighed with resignation. "I guess it might be a good idea to get it checked."

He nodded. "It is a good idea. And I know it was, because it was my idea."

"Don't be a donkey."

Saint chuckled. "Your idea of profanity is hilarious."

"I'm serious."

"So am I." He met her gaze, then realized his hand was still on her arm. *No loitering, Captain.* He cleared his throat. "This is going to seem like a strange request, but would you like to go to a party tonight?"

Brooke blanched. "What?"

"It's my birthday, and my mum's throwing me a small get-together. Mostly my family, really. I just don't feel comfortable leaving you two here alone."

"Oh, gosh, Captain, I don't know . . ."

"Just think about it. Not a big deal. I can cancel it," he said, forcing himself to keep his hands in his pockets lest he ruin his hair or try to cover his embarrassment.

"Oh, no, don't cancel. No reason why we should ruin your weekend, too, right?" Her throat moved as she swallowed hard. "Your mum really won't mind?"

"Shall I call her and check?"

"Yes. Please do. If she approves, we'll go."

He dialed as Brooke took off her outer layers. "Hi, Mum," he said in Imaharan. It was rude to do so in front of Everleigh, but his mum really did prefer it. "Can I bring two more tonight?"

"Of course," she said. "Did Edward's plans change?"

"No, he's still out of town. This is Brooke and her son, Olly, the boy I've been mentoring. I told you about them, remember?" Their names stuck out comically in the stream of Imaharan, like a soprano hitting a high note.

"Yes, I remember."

"Their apartment was vandalized, so they're staying with me until she can have it checked for curses and get her locks fixed."

"Of course they are welcome to join us. There will be lots of food. They must come. You didn't need to ask."

"You know how Orangiersians are. She doesn't want to come without an invitation."

"Aren't you Orangiersian?" she teased, and he laughed.

"Only part of me is. I don't know what I am now. Imaharsian, maybe. Orangieharan?"

She laughed. "Let me speak to her, please."

"Okay, hang on." He switched it to speakerphone as they both switched languages to Common Tongue. "Go ahead."

"Brooke?"

"Saint's mum?"

Saint could hear his mum's smile in her voice. "Yes, I am his mum. We would like for you to come tonight, you and your son. We would be honored to have you."

"Thank you so much; we'll be there. I hope it's not an inconvenience."

"Not at all. We'll see you tonight. Don't be too early."

"That won't be a problem with these two in tow, I assure you . . . ," Saint replied.

"Love you, son."

"Love you, too, Mum." He hung up.

Brooke crossed her arms. "Did you coerce her? You did a lot of talking before she spoke to me."

"Yes, I did. I told her you were very high maintenance and demanded to be involved in our celebration."

"Donkey," Brooke said, whacking him in the chest, and he laughed.

"She wants you to come, Brooke. It's fine, really."

"And they all speak Common Tongue?"

He nodded. The comment irked him a little, but he reminded himself that not everyone interacted with minorities as much as he did. "Does that surprise you? They live here, don't they?"

Brooke blushed. "I don't know, I just thought . . ."

"Mum is the least proficient, since she mostly hangs out with Imaharans, but you'll have no trouble conversing with anyone."

She nodded, but he thought she still didn't seem at all sure this was a good idea. "I'm sorry if I'm asking a lot of questions . . ."

He waved her off. "It's fine."

"Can I ask one more?" He loved this side of her. The side that wanted to dig into a story, find a connection.

He grinned. "Can I stop you?"

Brooke rolled her eyes, then sobered. "What was it like growing up in an Imaharan family?"

Saint crossed his arms. "It was good. I can't speak for all Imaharan families, obviously, but the Makis have a strong sense of cooperation, a healthy dependence and 'family first' kind of feeling to their life. They're part of this amazing, supportive expatriate community, but they never made me feel like an outsider. My siblings don't bring up too often that my first name doesn't start with *H* like all of theirs," he said with a wink.

She smiled. "I'm glad you had them in your life."

"So am I. In a very real sense, they saved me." Feeling the emotion clogging his throat, Saint coughed. "We'll go after you get back from doing the police report. Okay?"

"Okay."

TO A WOMAN WITH NO siblings, it seemed like there were a lot of names to know in Saint's family.

"This is my dad, Atsuki. He goes by Art."

"Great to meet you, Art. Olly loves to draw, he'll probably be fascinated with your name." Everyone laughed, but Brooke cringed. *That was a dumb joke, and probably offensive.*

"And my mum, Fuyumi. She goes by Juniper."

"It is easier," she explained. "Many people here, they cannot say 'Fuyumi,' so I chose another name." She shrugged. "Easier."

"Yes, I understand," said Brooke, thinking that she wouldn't want her name butchered all the time, either, but also thinking how ridiculous it was that people couldn't learn to pronounce it correctly. "It is so sweet of you to include us in the celebration, thank you so much for having us."

"Oh, we are honored to have you," she said, smiling. "So many people already, two more is nothing."

"And you already know Hanae."

"Mrs. Foster." She hadn't realized that Saint and the principal were related until now, but it did make a few things start to fall into place.

"Lovely to have you with us, Ms. Everleigh." *Now she remembers the* miss . . .

"Oh, please, call me Brooke."

"And this is her husband, Will."

"Nice to meet you, Brooke."

Olly had run off somewhere with Saint's nieces and nephews, but she couldn't chase him because there were still more adults for her to meet. *Hurry up, people. Broken glass does not make for a happy birthday.* She needed eyes on Olly again ASAP.

"And this is Hideo, Hitoshi, and my little brother, Hinata, the restauranteur," Saint said, the pride in his voice unmistakable.

Brooke nodded to each in turn. "Great to meet you all."

"Likewise," said Hinata, stepping forward to shake her hand. "Come by the restaurant sometime. You can write an article about it and get a free dinner at the same time." He winked at her.

"Perhaps I will." She smiled.

"We have some time before dinner," Art said. "Shall we play a game?"

"You know," Saint said, "it is *my* birthday . . ." The younger adults began to banter with him, Imaharan and Common Tongue overlapping, and Brooke found herself grinning at the obvious affection in the group. Art held up his hands for silence.

"Francis? What were you saying?"

"Did I say we had to play basketball? Did I say that?" Saint asked, and the others just shook their heads, muttering. "I was just trying to point out that since we've got Olly, we've got even teams for adults vs. kids . . ."

"I like the idea," said Art, and the others nodded begrudgingly. "Fuyumi, how long until pizza?"

"Half an hour, the man said."

"And the oven is on for the veggie pizza we brought, right?" Saint asked.

"Right."

He clapped a hand on her shoulder, and she jumped. "That's for you. And Everleigh, I know you're not sporty, so you get to keep score for us." He handed her a small whiteboard and a marker.

She took it and saluted, making him grin at her crookedly. *Golly, that's a nice look on him.* They stood staring at each other for a long moment, and Brooke felt the same irresistible attraction to him that she'd felt earlier in the day. *Like two poles of a darn magnet.*

"Okay," Art said, "let's go outside and play."

She followed the group to the front door, where she'd left her shoes, and started to carry them to the back door, where she could see the basketball hoop out on the patio. A gentle hand touched her shoulder, and she turned to see Hanae shaking her head. She tipped her head toward the front door, and Brooke realized everyone else had gone out the front to avoid having shoes in the house at all. She grinned at Hanae, a silent thank you for not revealing her faux pas, and she grinned back. Olly had already followed suit, and she was relieved that he was better than she was at taking his cues from the others.

"First team to twenty wins." Saint assumed a little more of his usual bossiness when they got to the basketball court, which was clearly his domain. "Mum, Brooke, you might want to stay up there where it's safe. It's gonna get wild down here."

She hopped up and sat on the edge of the deck, whiteboard still in hand, enjoying the feel of the cold as it nipped at her nose and fingers.

"You act as if we might break," Fuyumi said, leaning against the railing next to her. "I raised you to know better." Her face transformed as a quiet joy overtook her, watching her children and grandchildren organizing themselves.

"Oh"—Saint came running up to Brooke—"and hold my phone." Then he took off back toward the hoop mounted on the shed.

"Why do you say such things?" his mum asked. "Is it her job to serve you?"

"She doesn't mind, do you?" he called back, grinning.

"Such confidence," Fuyumi said, shaking her head.

"He hasn't always been like this?" Brooke asked.

"Oh, no," Fuyumi laughed. "No, no. The military gave him that."

"What was he like as a child?"

She was quiet for so long, Brooke wasn't sure she'd heard her question. "He was angry. Very angry. When he came to us, we thought, 'All he needs is some love, and he will settle down.'" She shook her head. "It was not so." Brooke felt bad that she'd made her so sad.

"What happened?"

"Some people did not support our decision to adopt a child who was so different from us. Friends distanced themselves, though they would not say why. We tried many things to make him happy. We read books, tried different ways to help him learn to control himself. None of it worked. Finally, we found an adoption support group. They told us about reactive attachment disorder."

Brooke cocked her head. "What is that? I've never heard of it."

Fuyumi shook her head. "It is common, but we did not know about it, either. The group, they said that because his mother neglected him, he will be angry a long time, maybe forever." She took a sip of her water. "It was very difficult. Perhaps more difficult for us, because where we come from, being so disrespectful, shouting, is dishonorable. But it was his way."

"I'm so sorry, Fuyumi," Brooke said, stumbling over the name a tiny bit, but laying a hand on her arm. "How did you get through it?"

"I quit my accounting work to spend more time with him. Every day, I would hold him while he watched TV. At first, he does not like it, but he got used to it. He began to accept it. He began to want it. He was still very skeptical about us. His father had to work even harder than I did. Francis liked basketball, so they played every day. Hours, they played. Step by step, he learned to trust us. We had to be so patient, we had to love him so unconditionally, far beyond what we thought we could do. School was still hard for him, for many years. But the military was good. It gave him the structure he wanted, the discipline. Seeing him now? It was worth it." Fuyumi covered Brooke's hand with her own on the edge of the deck and gave it a light squeeze. "I tell you this story because I believe you will understand, because I believe you want to understand. I know that you too know what it feels like to struggle, to fight. Francis has told us that you fight for what is good."

Brooke opened her mouth, but nothing came out. *He said that about me?*

"Trust is still difficult for him, Brooke. He knows many people, many women, but they do not know him. He mentors many children, but once the program is finished, he does not see them again. For many years, he allows no new attachments, no real bond." She turned her gaze back to the yard, where Saint obviously muffed a pass so the kids could steal the ball. "I like to see him with your son. I think he would be a good father."

"So do I," Brooke said. *Is she giving me her blessing?* She wanted to squirm; his mum was getting the wrong idea about them entirely. This was a tentative friendship at best—there was no sense in getting her hopes up.

"Of course, I am sure most mothers would think so. We are biased, aren't we, when it comes to our boys?"

"Very." She grinned. "And it doesn't help when good men like your son come along and confirm my opinion that my son is a sweet kid who's full of potential, even if no one else can see it."

"Oh, I also can see it. He is just finding his way. He will find it. We will help."

"I would love that," Brooke whispered.

"My son is very happy, being with you. He may not show it, but I know."

She reddened. "Oh, Fuyumi, I hope we haven't given you the wrong impression, Francis and I aren't . . . I mean, we're helping Olly together, but we're not . . ."

"Mothers know things, Brooke. You are helping him. He will get there."

Brooke hopped down. "I think I'll just go pop my pizza in the oven . . ."

Something in her pocket started ringing, and she pulled it out. *Orangiers Correctional Facility 006, Women's Division.*

"Um, Saint? I think you're going to want to take this . . ."

He trotted over to her and answered. He put one finger in his other ear, moving away from the game still happening as the big kids took turns lifting Olly up to help him make a basket.

"Uh-huh. Yes, okay. Thank you. I will." He hung up, weaving his fingers together behind his head, walking around the side of the house.

As if drawn by a string, Brooke trailed after him. "Everything okay?" she asked softly.

"Calynda's been arrested again." He kicked an empty bucket, then braced his hands against the side of the house, breathing heavily. "Whatever. Let's play." He started past her.

"Saint." She stopped him with a light hand on his arm. "Do you want to talk about it?"

"If I don't do feelings talk on a normal day, I definitely don't do it on my birthday," he reprimanded gently, edging by her and returning to the game.

CHAPTER SEVENTEEN

A WEEK LATER, BROOKE was going over her to do list on Saturday morning.

> ~~- Have apartment checked for curses.~~
> ~~- Call Tezza Simonson about protective warding referral~~
> ~~- Replace doorknob~~
> ~~- Catalogue what was taken for police report~~
> - *Knit for Christmas*
> - *Pay bills*
> - *Regular cleaning*
> - *Post-break-in cleaning*

She'd saved the worst for last, unfortunately; the rest had been taken care of relatively quickly, thanks to Captain Saint's help. She wasn't sad when a knock at her door interrupted her procrastination.

"Morning, Everleigh." Saint, James and Simonson stood at her door with a bucket, empty water balloons, and a baseball bat.

"Hi," she said, holding back the giant grin that wanted to break through. She'd met the other two men at the birthday party last weekend, so she felt no hesitance in teasing them. "You realize this is doing nothing for my opinion that you're all just little boys in men's bodies?"

Saint grinned . . . *Is he blushing?*

"Sadly for you, love," said James, "all my affections are poured out upon my princess or I'd take it upon myself to change your mind."

"I'll try not to consider it a personal tragedy," Brooke replied.

Saint lowered the volume of his voice. "Any update on the break-in?"

She shook her head. "Based on the symbols and the slurs, they're Lincoln's supporters, but beyond that? My building doesn't have any cameras, and the police said no one saw anything. I'm sure *someone* did see, but I understand why they don't want to get involved . . . I don't blame them. I might have done the same."

"You? Ms. Do-Right? I don't think so," Saint said, a crooked smile on his face.

Brooke blushed. "Why are you here?"

"We're headed to Bluffton to play water balloon baseball on the big field. We've made a few improvements to the game, and we wanted to show Olly."

At the sound of his name, Olly came running to the front door, his eyes wide.

"Captain!" Upon noticing the bats and the buckets, his voice went up an octave. "Mum, can I go with him? Please? Please please please please . . ."

James and Saint joined in his cajoling.

"Please, Mum? Oh, please? Come on, Mum . . ."

Grinning, she waved her hands for silence from the barrage of whining. Brooke turned to her son. "You were supposed to fold those towels and pick up your room today."

His face fell, thinking. "Can you wait? I'll be lightning quick."

Sam's voice came through from the back. "At a minimum, you'd have to travel 136,000 miles per hour to manage that. I doubt you're that fast."

"I am!" he insisted. "I'm super fast!" He looked up at Saint, his eyes pleading. "Will you wait?"

Saint gave a dramatic sigh that made Brooke smirk. "Military man without his chores done by 10 a.m.? We've got some work to do on you, mate. But yes, we'll wait. Be quick about it." His eyes came to hers. "May we come in?"

Oh sugar. "Of course." She tried her best to ignore their reaction to the chaos. Olly tore through the flat, vaulting himself over debris, and disappeared down the hall. Brooke touched her hair self-consciously; it was still covered with a handkerchief to keep the dust off as she tried to put her place back together. Not knowing what else to do, she went back to the mess she'd put off cleaning for a week.

"Brooke, this place is still a disaster." Saint sounded angry. *No surprise there.* "Why didn't you call me to come help you with this stuff?"

She shrugged. "Because you're neither my boyfriend nor my brother." *And after such a wonderful weekend pretending to be a family, I needed a break from you.*

"But I'm your friend." With a head jerk, he signaled to James to help him right a bookshelf against the wall.

"Don't do that."

They ignored her.

"I'm serious, Saint. Stop it."

Olly came running out into the living room. "Done."

"That was suspiciously fast," Brooke said, crossing her arms. "Show me."

He scowled at her. "I'll pick up later. I did the towels . . ."

"No, you'll do it all now, or I'll send them on without you."

He opened his mouth to argue again, but Saint interrupted him. "Olly. Listen to your CO. She calls the shots." Olly turned and marched back to his room. As annoyed as she was with Saint, it was nice to have someone back her up for once. James and Sam started returning books to the shelf as Saint edged through the mess over to her.

"It's not a sin to need help, you know. Everyone does."

"Oh? I've yet to see you need any."

He grumbled something under his breath, but she didn't catch it.

"I beg your pardon, Captain?"

"Stop being so Woz-damn stubborn. This isn't a lead you're chasing. Why isn't Judson over here helping you? Where's your mum? Or your cousin?"

"I didn't ask for their help."

"Why the Jersey not?"

"Because I'm fine," she said, her tone firm.

"Oh, I'm sorry—were you bitten by a radioactive spider? Are you secretly from another planet? Because that's the only way in Jersey you were going to get that bookshelf back against the wall by yourself." He stalked down the hall, and she shot a wide-eyed look at his friends, who were clearly holding back amusement. Her heart rate ticked up.

"Where do you think you're going? Hey! Captain, get back here," she shouted after him, pounding down the hall. Brooke found him in her bedroom, going through her closet. "What the jackrabbit do you think you're doing?"

"I'm looking for your spandex suit and cape. It's got to be here somewhere."

She crossed her arms. "Very funny. Now get out of my bedroom."

He turned to face her and crossed his arms. "Not until I find your superhero costume. I bet it's smashing."

"Oh," she said, getting behind him, "there will be smashing if you don't get out of my bedroom, but I doubt it's the kind you prefer." She pushed him toward the door, but he didn't move more than an inch or two. He laughed. Brooke lowered her shoulder and shoved against his hip, trying to not ogle his backside. *Useless. This is useless. But he is going to respect my privacy . . .*

Game time was over. Brooke strode calmly out of the room and to the front door. She picked up the baseball bat where he'd left it. Then, ignoring his gaping friends, she strode back into the bedroom with it over her shoulder. He'd turned back to the closet and was sifting through it.

"How come I never see you wearing any of this? You've got some cute stuff in here."

Because I never lost that last ten pounds after being pregnant, you donkey.

"Get out of here, Captain. This is the last time I ask nicely."

"What are you—" He doubled over laughing. His friends, however, had seen the murderous look in her eye and were hovering nervously in the doorway.

"Are you going to let us do all the cleanup out there our-selves, lazybones? Come on, come help us." Brooke and Saint both ignored James's pleasant attempt to intervene.

"Are you trying to threaten me, Everleigh?" He stepped closer to her. "You realize I could disarm you easily, right? I've at least a hundred pounds on you. What do you think you're going to do to me?"

Brooke was shaking with rage. "You're a bully."

He blinked. "What?"

"You heard me. You're a bully. You don't care that I'm un-comfortable and unhappy that you're in here. You want to poke around in my space, so you're doing it."

"Brooke . . ." He ran a hand through his hair. "I was just try-ing to make a point."

"What? That I'm weak and you're strong? I'm painfully aware of that. Everyone seems to be stronger than me. But in here? I'm king and queen both. And if I want to let the book-shelf lie on the floor a few more days while I process the in-fringement of my sovereignty, I'll do that. And if I want to re-pair my sense of self by nailing my desk drawers back together myself, I'll do that." She stepped closer, mere inches from his stony face. "And if I tell you to leave my bedroom, then that's what you'll do, even if I have to convince you with a pathetic show of force. It seems to be the only language you understand, Captain."

"Mum?" The timidity in Olly's voice told her that he'd heard her speech, and she cringed.

"Yes, love?"

"I'm all done cleaning my room. Can I go now?"

"Yes, love."

"You're still letting him go?" Saint muttered, his eyes never leaving her face.

"I'm only as good as my word."

He stared at her a minute longer, then gave a single nod, gently pushing past her to the door. She closed her eyes to rebuff the tears collecting in the corners of her eyes and released a shaky breath. *Olly needs men in his life. Deserves it. Even when that man is acting like a bastard today for some reason.*

Saint was helping Olly into his coat, and she quickly grabbed a few granola bars from the kitchen to stick in his pockets.

"There's a snack if you're hungry. Don't con the Captain into buying you treats."

Olly still seemed unsure, and she kissed the top of his head and bent to look into his eyes. "It's okay, love. Mum lost her temper, that's all. Have a fun time, all right? Come home soaked." He grinned then, and she grinned back. "I love you, my sweet son."

"Love you, Mum."

She stood up. The three men were still standing in the doorway. "What are you waiting for?"

"We need our bat back," Sam mumbled, not making eye contact. "Please." She reddened; she'd forgotten she was still holding it. She passed it to Saint, who brushed her fingers with his as he took it, sending tingles up her arm.

"When would you like him home?" he asked.

"Three would be fine."

Single nod again. "Thank your mum for letting you come out with us, mate."

"Thanks, Mum," Olly called. He pointed at her with both hands, and she mirrored the gesture back to him. It was their silly thing: their secret handshake. Saint hung back as the others started down the stairs. She pinned him with a stare, daring him to argue with her again. *I don't have the bat anymore. Damn.* But something in his crestfallen expression told her she wouldn't need it . . .

"I'm sorry, Everleigh. I just . . ." He trailed off. "I'm sorry. I'll have him home on time."

"Okay."

CHAPTER EIGHTEEN

"YOU SHOULD'VE SEEN it, Edward," Arron James said around the sandwich he was eating. "It was unlike anything I've ever seen. He's so smitten with this woman. And she leveled him like . . . like . . ."

"Like an atomic weapon," Sam Simonson put in.

James swallowed. "I was going to say a volcano, but I like your thing better."

"But a volcano spews lava, and there were definitely flames happening. Yours is good, too."

"Thank you."

"You're welcome."

"Shut it, both of you," Saint growled. "I'm not *smitten*."

Simonson and James shared a look.

"I thought she was going to murder you with that baseball bat, and you just stood there with moony eyes," James said. "If that isn't love, I don't know what is."

"You're both idiots."

Edward said nothing, to Saint's mild surprise. His friend didn't usually hesitate to join in on a good ribbing, but Edward just sat and watched Abbie and Tezza play tag with Olly on Bluffton's south field; all the women found him adorable. *He is pretty adorable. A handful, but adorable.*

"Oh yes," James laughed, "we're the idiots. Not the man going after a woman who told him she didn't want him the moment she met him. That's not insensible at all."

"Perhaps it's for the best, as your relationship would be doomed from its inception," Edward said.

Saint lifted his head to give his friend a hard stare. "Who's talking right now?"

Edward's eyebrows snapped together, low on his forehead. "Pardon?"

"Are you my boss or my friend right now? I can't tell."

Slowly, Edward turned to Arron and Sam. "Would you two excuse us, just for a moment?"

"I believe I'd like to stay," Arron said. Sam began dragging him down the bleachers by the collar. "Seems like an interesting conversation is about to take place. I think I'd—hey, Simonson, let go of me. I can walk on my own, thank you very much."

"You were saying?" Saint prompted, arms crossed over his chest, sunglasses faithfully hiding his eyes and therefore the emotions crawling to the surface.

"I'm uncertain why we're even having this conversation. You can't date a reporter."

"Why? I'm not her boss."

"Why?" Edward echoed, shaking his head. "Because it's still favoritism. Every time you call on her in the briefing room, the other reporters are going to resent it. Every time she breaks a story first, they're going to say it was pillow talk. Every time she goes after my administration, because this likely won't be the last instance of that, it's going to make you look bad. And by extension, make me look bad." Edward balled up the parchment paper his sandwich had been wrapped in and calmly stood. "I looked the other way when you bedded Scrope and Paris and all the rest, but I can't this time. I think it's fantastic that you're mentoring her son, investing in the life of a boy who needs a father figure. Just don't forget that you can't stand in his father's shoes when it comes to his mother. You've always excelled at finding other outlets for those impulses, anyway; no shortage of ladies in line to have a piece of Saint."

He was trying to make him laugh. He had just shut down any possibility of him getting together with Everleigh and keeping his job, and he was making a Woz-damn *joke*. Saint started his meditative breathing without realizing he was doing it. *In for four, hold for seven, out for eight. In for four . . .*

"And to answer your question, I am always your friend. You're good at this job, Saint. Very good. I don't want to see you screw that up over a pointless fling." He clapped him on the shoulder as he descended the bleachers, and it felt like a slap to the face rather than the back.

CHAPTER NINETEEN

AFTER HIS CONVERSATION with Edward, Saint decided to keep his distance from Everleigh. It seemed like the easiest way to stave off more feelings. A few weeks went by, and they didn't share anything more than passing greetings as they exchanged Olly. But when Saint went to sit down to watch TV on the evening of their latest meeting and saw Olly's backpack, he decided to walk it over. No sense in getting him in trouble with Hanae or his teacher needlessly. It had nothing to do with missing Brooke, he told himself.

Saint knocked on her door, and it took a long time for her to come. Worry crept in that she'd had another home invasion, this time when she was present . . . He'd just raised his hand to knock again harder when she opened the door.

"Hey."

"Hey," she echoed, but she didn't smile.

"He left his backpack, I thought perhaps he'd need it tomorrow . . ."

She nodded, leaning against the doorjamb. "Thank you." Something was off.

"Everything all right?" She nodded, avoiding his gaze, biting her lips.

No, it's not.

"Want to come in?"

"Just for a minute . . ."

The house was cleaner than usual, and there was a quarter of a bottle of red wine on the island. "You want a drink?"

"Sure." He watched her as she poured. *Definitely something off.* "You drink all that yourself?"

She gave an exaggerated nod, and he noticed how pink her nose was. She topped off her own glass with the rest of it, killing the bottle.

"Maybe go easy on that stuff, Everleigh. It's only Wednesday, you know."

She laughed, low and throaty. "It is only Wednesday, that's true. Too bad shit can happen any day of the week."

"What shit? Wait, *shit*? You actually used a bad word." He looked around. "Where's Olly?"

"He's with my cousin, Rachel."

"Why?"

She shrugged, looking at the ceiling. "I wanted to be alone."

He put down his glass. "What happened?"

"First of all, my stupid microwave stopped working again. I tried to talk to it, you know, person to magical appliance, but I swear it growled at me, so I had to make grilled cheese for dinner and I burned it, of course . . . And then my smoke detector didn't even go off, so I think all the devices are conspiring against me, and then my phone rang, and it was . . ." She let her head fall back, still looking at the ceiling. Her sigh was wet and shaky. "Why did I even answer?" She took another big swallow of her wine. "Why did I answer the phone?"

"Who called you?"

"Charlie." She whispered the name.

He covered her hand with his, about to ask who Charlie was, when he realized he might already know. *I'm Oliver Charles Everleigh . . .*

"Olly's dad? He called you? What did he want?"

"He wants partial custody." She looked into his eyes, and he saw how devastated she was. "And I can't fight him. He has money. I don't have money." She rested her forehead on his bicep. "Woz, you're strong. Will you beat up Charlie for me? I don't have money, I can't pay you."

He would've laughed if she hadn't said it so brokenly. Saint made the executive decision that she was done drinking and shifted both wine glasses away from her. He wrapped an arm around her and pressed her to his side.

"Hey," he said softly. "You'll get through this. Maybe he'll change his mind."

She shook her head, her voice thick with unshed tears. "He's already got a barrister. I'm jacked." Brooke covered her face with both of her hands and sobbed. Saint wrapped her tightly in his arms.

"Love, what can I do?"

"Nothing," she mumbled, sniffling. "You can't . . ." She hiccupped. "You can't do anything."

"There must be something. Do you want me to take Olly overnight so you can talk to Charlie without him around?"

She looked up at him, and the earnestness was palpable. "You like Olly, don't you?"

"Of course I do, he's a great kid."

"And me?"

He wiped the mascara trails from under her eyes tenderly, fumbling internally for the right thing to say. "You too. You're both very important to me." Her eyes went hot, molten, and her gaze dropped to his lips. That was all the warning he got before her hands were on his face, pulling him toward her, kissing him like her life depended on it. Saint froze for a moment, but his indecision was embarrassingly short-lived. He pressed his body to hers like any distance between them was a crime, pinning her against the island. Her hands were everywhere: threading through his hair, caressing under his shirt, tracing the tips of his ears, squeezing his backside through his jeans. His thoughts were swimming like he was the one who was drunk, his ego proudly floating on its back in the middle of it all . . . until he tasted the wine on her breath. *Oh, right.* His conscience pulled the drain plug.

"Wait . . ." He drew back, but she followed him, pushing him onto the barstool and moving between his parted legs. "Brooke, wait a minute . . ." Her nipples grazed his chest through their shirts, and he thought his eyes were going to roll back in his head permanently with pleasure.

"I want you," she whispered, kissing his neck. "Take me to bed, Captain. That's an order." She tilted her hips forward into him eagerly.

He groaned so loud, he felt it in his sternum. "Tonight's not the night for this, love." He realized to his shame that he was still kissing her; he didn't exactly know how to stop. How did one give up a willing woman who was clearly ready for anything? He forced himself to pull away, panting, pressing their foreheads together. Her hands went to her shirt buttons.

"I know you've been dying to handle these . . ." The slightest hint of lace had him salivating. He lifted a hand to touch her, but pulled back as though burned.

"Brooke . . . you said you didn't want this, remember? Let's take a step back." Apparently, his libido was controlling everything but his mouth. She stepped back, and he let out a relieved sigh . . . until she dropped to her knees in front of him, her fingers popping free the button of his jeans. He swore.

"Brooke, stop, Woz-condemn-it! If you were sober, you wouldn't be doing this. You told me no; you told me never. You're just scared, you're just sad." He hauled her back up to her feet and held her tightly against his chest, even though his heart was still beating wildly. Without letting her go, he walked her backwards down the hall. "You just need sleep, love."

"Yes, orgasm-induced sleep," she purred.

"No, regular sleep," he said, using his commander voice. "It'll all look better in the morning."

"You're going to do me again in the morning? Lovely. Olly's not here, we won't get caught. We can be as loud as we want." That did give him pause. He was giving up an opportunity here . . . a rare opportunity. But the friendship . . . it was tenuous enough without adding this. *This is the right thing to do,* he told himself. *For her sake.* She tried to wiggle out of his hold, and he groaned.

"I hope you have the world's worst hangover, you wicked woman. I've got at least one beloved body part that isn't going to speak to me after this." He threw her onto the bed and retreated before she could grab him again. Brooke pouted, kicking her feet, before she turned over into the pillow, sighing.

"So handsome," she murmured. "So sweet. Would've been so good . . ."

"You'll thank me tomorrow," he grumbled, hightailing it back down the hall before she could wake up and change her mind.

CHAPTER TWENTY

IN THE LIGHT OF EARLY morning, Brooke stumbled into the bathroom to confirm that there was no hammer sticking out of her head. It certainly felt like there was; the pounding was very uncomfortable. She popped two ibuprofen dry, then went for coffee. She leaned over on the kitchen island to wait for it to brew, scrolling through her social media feeds. Empty red wine bottle (that added up), two wine glasses . . .

Wait, two glasses? Who else could've . . . Surely she hadn't called Charlie. No, she wouldn't have done that. *Judson hates wine.* She scanned the room for more clues: a jacket or hat left behind perhaps . . . Her eyes landed on Olly's backpack. Which should've been with Olly, but he'd left it with . . . Saint.

Oh no. No, no, no.

Memories flooded back to her as she ran to the bathroom, looking for evidence of sex and/or contraception. *I started it; he was surprised. I ran my hands through his silky hair, his hot mouth sucked on my bottom lip, he groaned when I unbuttoned my shirt . . .* But there was nothing in the trash can, on the bathroom counter, or by the bed. That could be good. She cringed. *But I need to know for sure . . .*

She picked up her phone to call him and was startled to hear someone clear his throat just outside her door. Regardless of the fact that she was still in her pajamas, she opened the door and peeked out, only to squeak her surprise.

There was a soldier out there. A big one. But it was not Saint.

"Who are you? What are you doing outside my door?" The shrillness of her own voice made her cringe, and her headache ratcheted up another notch.

"I'm Corporal Harrison. Captain Saint asked me to stand guard here because of your recent break-in. He left a note." He handed her an envelope, and she went back inside before tearing it open.

B—

I had to have someone stand guard because I didn't have a key to lock up when I left. You were already asleep. He'll be off duty now that you're awake.

—S

She dialed.

"This is Captain Saint."

"Hi, it's me, it's Brooke."

She could hear him grinning. "Good morning," he said. "How's your head?"

"It . . . hurts." She paused, unsure of what to say next. "Thanks for the note."

"Sure." She really should've planned out what to say so she didn't blurt out, *So, attractive male friend, did I jump you last night by chance?* Time was lapsing again . . .

"Did you need something?"

"No. Sorry. Well, yes, sorry, I guess I do . . . I'm sorry to ask this, but did we . . . last night, did we . . . I couldn't find a . . ." She sighed.

"We didn't."

"We didn't?" she whispered. "But I remember squeezing your . . . I knelt down and grabbed your . . ."

"Yes, you did. But that's as far as it went. I put you to bed and left." Relief ripped through her, and she silently thanked whatever deity had given him more self-control than her.

"Sorry, I don't think I heard you right, Captain Sinner. You took me to bed, correct?"

He laughed. "*Put* you to bed. You were drunk, love. Didn't mean what you were saying."

Dread gripped her like a child being dropped off at daycare. "What did I say? Did I talk about your backside? Oh, Woz . . ."

"No, you didn't," he chuckled. "But by all means, go ahead . . ."

"Captain, please forgive me. I should never have put you in that position."

"Love, aren't you listening? I said you didn't get me into bed, there were no positions involved."

"Saint," she said, straining to keep her voice even, "please don't joke. Please. I'm so very sorry. Please don't think less of me, please don't tell anyone . . ."

That sobered him. "I've not told a soul. Your secret is safe with me."

"Thank you," she whispered. "And thank you for . . . stopping."

"You're welcome. I've got to prepare for the briefing. See you then?"

"Yes. Okay."

"Bye, love."

"Bye."

But I did mean it, Brooke thought as she finished her coffee. *I meant it all. Maybe he's not into me after all . . .* In a daze, Brooke got dressed, did her makeup, and packed her messenger bag. She stopped for more coffee on her way to the train. The shop was crowded, so how she noticed them, she couldn't later recall. Something about their red jackets, their menacing stares, had caught her eye. She paid for her short dark roast with milk and turned from the counter just in time to see them approach. There were three of them, all white men, and the tallest one was clearly the leader.

"You're that woman, the reporter."

Brooke didn't answer. Using her elbow, she attempted to push past them, but they blocked her way.

"Hey, I'm talking to you. What's your problem with the king, anyway? He's a decent sort—unlike you."

"Look," she gritted out, "I made a mistake, okay? It happens."

"Maybe the public should be protected from your kind of mistakes."

"Better to make a mistake in the service of justice than to keep my mouth shut and watch it happen."

"But it wasn't justice, was it?" He shoved her shoulder. The coffee sloshed onto her coat, and she shook the hot liquid off her hand, stinging from the burn.

"Get out of my way," Brooke enunciated, "or I'll call the police."

Begrudgingly, the leader stepped aside, and she bolted for the door, digging for her phone in her bag.

"Judson." She tried to keep the tears out of her voice, but he heard them anyway.

"What's happened? Is Olly okay?"

She nodded, despite it being a phone call. "He's fine, he's good. Can you meet me at the train station nearest Bluffton?

Something's happened, and I can't . . ." She lowered her voice. "I can't walk alone right now."

"Right. Yes, right, I'll be right there."

"Wait a few minutes; I have a stop to make. I'll text you when I'm close."

"All right, love. Be safe, please."

"Yes, I will." She was in luck for once; the sporting goods store had one more tiny black canister of pepper spray. Brooke tucked it into the outside pocket of her bag and boarded the train, but she couldn't seem to let go of it.

CHAPTER TWENTY-ONE

IT WAS ONLY A FEW DAYS before the holiday break, and it was their last meeting with Saint. It was a relief, of course, Brooke told herself as she slid a pepperoni and green pepper pizza into the oven. Good to have this over and done with. Since he'd been coming over on weekends, it was easy to get their required hours in more quickly. Frankly, she didn't mind her neighbors seeing a military man around; the people who'd graffitied her door and trashed the place were probably still watching her, still pissed at her for ruining their plans. The exiled prince had a surprising number of loyal followers . . . but maybe having Saint around would convince Lincoln's supporters to leave her alone.

She'd work while they played video games or drew at the kitchen table or went to the park if it wasn't too cold. Not that there had been a lot of work to do lately—no one trusted her with their story. No one wanted to collaborate at work. It was like she was cursed, and she wasn't sure how to break it.

Still, she'd been going through her traditional battery of Christmas shirts in the lead-up to the holiday—the best day of the year—and today's was a particular favorite: "Gangsta Wrapper," with a roll of red and green wrapping paper and a pair of scissors on it. There was a knock, and she hurried to answer it; Mrs. Cavanaugh could go suck an egg. Saint groaned when he saw her shirt.

"Another one?"

She nodded, grinning. "Come in."

"I like this one better than 'Tree Rex,'" he said. "That poor dinosaur was all tangled," he said, imitating the creature that had been wrapped in lights and garlands on her shirt.

"I'm sure he got free eventually," she said. "Olly! Captain Saint's here!"

"Coming!" he called back, and the adults shared an amused look.

"What's he doing back there?" he asked, pointing.

"No idea. Come to think of it, it's been very quiet."

"Strange. Perhaps I should investigate . . . ," he said, shuffling toward the hallway.

"No, wait." She touched his arm, and he turned back to her. "I know this is our last meeting," she said in a rush, "and I just wanted to thank you, and I just wanted to see if you'd want to grab lunch with us next week. We'd love to see you." His mum's words about him breaking ties with his students pulsed inside her head, but she pressed on. "We just don't want to lose contact with you. I think it would be good for Olly to be able to touch base."

He arched an eyebrow at her, smirking. "You make it sound like we're closing some sort of business merger." He lowered his voice an octave. *"Let's keep the lines of communication open as we move forward."*

Olly came tearing down the hall then, and it was clear the conversation was over as they turned on the television and booted up the game console.

Oh well, she thought. *I tried.* But a sadness settled over her that even pizza couldn't shake. Saint groaned when she put the festive pizza she'd made on the table, and the guys polished it off quickly. She'd just started into hers when some movement out the window caught her eye.

"It's snowing," she said, awestruck. OIly knocked over his chair trying to get to the window first.

"Let's go out, Mum! Please?"

By the time he was appropriately bundled, snow lay on the ground like a blanket, fluffy but wet enough to pack firmly. They crossed the street to the public park. A snowman was first, of course, then Brooke allowed herself to be goaded into a snowball fight, boys against . . . woman.

"Everyone says, 'boys against girls,' Mum," Olly complained.

"I'm not a girl. I'm a woman. It can be boys against woman this time. If you're going to gang up on me, the least you can do is let me pick my moniker."

"Your what?" Saint called, teasing. "Your momiker?"

"Ha ha," she replied coolly, all the while quickly creating her stash, while they were busy talking strategy. If she was fast, it wouldn't matter that she was outnumbered. Arms full, she came around the play structure, enjoying the balance of Olly's surprised squeal and Saint's bellow.

"Dirty pool, we didn't say go!" yelled Saint. "Fine, if that's the way you want it . . ."

He tackled her into the snow, then held her down while Olly plundered her stash.

Brooke grinned up at him. "It was dirty, wasn't it?"

"I should've expected no less from you," he replied, his look censorious. Something in his eyes softened then, and he sat back on his heels. "Everleigh, I . . ." He gasped.

"Team Everleigh!" yelled Olly as he stuffed a snowball down Saint's back.

"Oh, a true loyalist!" Brooke cried, scrambling to her feet, trying not to guess what Saint had been about to say. "Well done, my sweet son!"

They lobbed snowballs over the structure at each other for another ten minutes or so until everyone was panting and soggy, and then she called it a draw.

"Go up and get started in the shower," she said to Olly, passing him the keys, kissing his snowy forehead, his cheeks rosy. "I'll be right up."

"Bye, Olly," Saint called as the boy crossed the street.

"Bye, Captain," he called back, waving. "I'll miss you."

Brooke felt tears clogging her throat, but she swallowed them down. "Well. I guess this is it."

"Yup. Guess so." They would see each other at work, of course, but it wasn't the same.

They stared at each other for a long moment before Brooke pulled off her glove and stuck out her hand. Pulling his own off with his teeth, he pressed his cold hand into hers, and they stood outside her apartment building, shaking hands. He began to pull back. Brooke intended to let go, but her fingers, affected by the cold no doubt, held on and she stumbled into his chest.

"Are you okay?" He braced his hands on her shoulders, looking into her eyes.

"Sorry, I . . . ," she muttered. "I'm sorry." Then she turned and fled into the building, red-cheeked, before he could say anything else.

THE NEXT MORNING, BROOKE was still walking Oliver to school when her phone rang, interrupting a story about how his new friend Harry had a cat with one green eye and one blue. It was her editor, Miranda.

"Good morning, Brooke. Do you have a moment?"

"Of course. What's on your mind?"

Miranda's deep sigh had Brooke's shoulders tensing up. "You're going to stay home today. I'm sending Patricia to the press briefing."

"Any particular reason?"

"Mum, look! Two squirrels chasing each other!" her son screeched, pulling on her coat sleeve.

She nodded to Olly, tapping one finger to her lips as a reminder to be quiet while she was on the phone.

"Our advertisers are pulling out. They want you gone. They don't want to appear to approve of a publication that slanders the king. I'm sorry. I've gone to bat for you, but we have to follow the money. That's reality."

Reality bites, she thought. Out loud, she said, "No, I understand. Thank you for trying."

"This is a tough business, and I thought you brought a lot to it. It's a shame it didn't work out."

"Yeah." Words didn't often fail her, but Brooke couldn't think of a single thing to say.

"We've put you on administrative leave through the end of the month. You can come clean out your desk next week."

And worst of all, I won't see Saint anymore. Not even in passing. And her heart could not be consoled by any other benefit that this turn of events might bring.

"Okay." The meekness in her own voice infuriated her, but she couldn't take it out on Miranda. It wasn't her fault; the blame fell squarely on her own shoulders.

"Take care, Brooke. Merry Christmas."

"You too," she whispered, as she kissed Olly goodbye at the edge of the schoolyard.

CHAPTER TWENTY-TWO

SAINT: Didn't see you at the briefing yesterday or today.

Brooke: Since I wasn't there, I can't say I'm surprised.

Saint: Everything okay?

Brooke: Just taking some time off.

He growled. He'd cornered Judson today at the briefing after she hadn't shown up two days in a row, worried that she was avoiding him following their awkward goodbye after the snowball fight . . . the moment he'd almost kissed her. He'd been saved by her clumsy stumble into his chest; he'd never have thought he'd be grateful for that quality. Boote admitted that she'd had a run-in with some pushy loyalists and said he'd planned to walk her to work . . . until she got fired.

Saint: When were you going to tell me about your run-in at the coffee shop?

Saint: And losing your job?

Brooke: Judson Boote is a dead man.

Saint: Let me see about a protective detail for you. Just for a few weeks.

Brooke: I'm fine, thanks. I can knock down a bear from 100 feet away.

Saint: You know that's not how pepper spray works, right?

Saint: I've got a tenner that says you blind yourself.

Brooke: I'd take that bet, but I haven't got a cent to spare on the off chance I'm wrong.

Saint: Seriously, though. You're all right?

Brooke: I am seriously all right.

He tucked his phone away and strode into the king's office. "Edward."

He looked up from his desk at Saint. "Yes?"

"We need to talk about your Christmas address."

"Sorry to interrupt, Your Majesty, but you're needed in the residence."

Edward blinked at Scrope as if she hadn't been speaking Common Tongue and his mind were translating. "I beg your pardon?" His hand went immediately to his phone, but there was no message.

"I said you're needed in the residence." Scrope, ever the picture of focus and professionalism, was smirking. *Smirking.*

"Can it wait?"

"Based on the posters, I'd say no."

"Posters?" Saint asked.

She handed him a sheet of paper that had been yellowed to look old, perhaps with coffee, as it smelled of it faintly. He skimmed it quickly, then burst out laughing. Saint handed it to his friend. Edward's eyes widened, then narrowed. They remained narrowed as he rose from his seat and began to stalk out of the office.

"Do you want me to follow, or . . ."

"Yes," he snapped, and Saint allowed himself a brief but satisfying crooked grin as he fell into step with him. But once the work talk started, he wiped it from his face.

"We have a rough draft going, but we wanted to see if there were any social issues or political situations you wanted to highlight during the address beyond the regular holiday platitudes."

"No, I don't think so. It'll be short this year. Just the general good wishes, a short recap of the country's successes in the last year . . ."

"Right. Twenty minutes?"

"Yes. No more than thirty, please. My voice starts to give out."

"Television and radio both? Live streaming?"

"All of the above."

"Abbie or no Abbie?"

Edward grumbled under his breath and reached out to open the door to the residence. It was locked. "That's looking unlikely at this exact moment."

He banged on the door with his fist.

"Abs, open up, for Woz's sake."

She answered the door serenely, then her face melted into exaggerated shock. "Wonderful Wozniack be praised, you're alive! You're *alive*!" She moved to embrace him, but he stepped back. He held up the poster next to his head as if she hadn't seen it, as if she hadn't designed it and hung it all over the palace offices.

"What is the meaning of this?"

"Golly, I couldn't say."

Edward went on undeterred, reading the poster's text. "Missing: one husband, black. Age: 23. Last seen wearing: a suit probably. Also answers to Parker, His Majesty or Sweet Cheeks."

She winked at Saint. "That's in reference to his backside, not his face, in case you were wondering."

"I wasn't," he answered, but he couldn't keep a grin off his face.

Edward shook the paper at her to regain her attention. "Where did you obtain this photograph of me?"

"I took it while you were asleep. I managed to catch you in bed with me a few nights ago. Since I hadn't seen you in three days, I thought I should seize the opportunity to remember what you look like." Abbie took the paper from him, admiring her own handiwork. "I thought it came out good."

"I'm drooling!"

"No one's perfect." She paused. "I missed you."

"There are other ways to express that!" he yelled, and based on experience, Saint knew he was more exasperated than truly angry.

"I tried those!" she yelled back, her voice tinged with desperation. "You weren't taking my calls, you don't answer my texts or my emails. I call Scrope, and she says you're in a meeting. I come down the hall to find you and you're not there." She edged closer to him. "I just want to eat with you," she said, her volume falling, the desperation holding firm. "I just want to see you and hear about your very busy day. I just want you to know that I care." Her last words were a whisper. "And know that you care about me."

Her words echoed Everleigh's so closely that Saint's brain went silent for a moment, contemplating what that might mean. *And she got all flustered and sad, and instead of saying "Yes, I'd love to do lunch," I took the coward's way out and made a joke. I brushed her off.*

Edward's eyes never left his wife's earnest face as he pulled out his phone.

"Scrope? Cancel whatever's happening this weekend. I'm going out of town with my wife." He listened. "No, *this* weekend. They'll just have to deal with it." He hung up. "Better?"

She nodded, smiling. "Still annoyed with me?"

He slid his jaw to the side. "Yes . . . but I'll just have to deal with it." He put his hands on his hips. "Go take those down before you go to class, will you? The tittering is going to get to me, and I don't need some dignitary seeing them by accident."

She held up her hands in innocence. "I only put them in office areas."

"Right, so only my *subjects and employees* will lose respect for me . . ."

Saint scoffed. "It just reminds them that you need a break. Maybe leave a few up." He stepped away and pulled out his phone as they continued to argue.

Saint: Still want to get lunch next week? My treat.

Brooke: Your busy schedule open up?

Saint: Something like that.

Saint: You in? You, me, Olly? I'll pick you up Saturday.

Brooke: Great, Olly'll be thrilled.

Brooke: But he's gonna want that medieval place.

Saint: Medieval Meats and More? That's fine.

Brooke: See you at 11:00.

Saint looked up to find Edward gone and Abbie staring at him.

"What?"

"You're beaming. Who are you flirting with?"

He tucked his phone into his pocket. "No one."

Abbie gave him an arch look and pulled him into the residence by his sleeve, closing the door softly. "Now tell me who."

Saint sighed. "It's Everleigh."

"The reporter? I thought all that was done with. Come sit."

He followed her over to the white marble kitchen island and sat down hard on a teal metal stool. "The crisis part is. The attraction part isn't." He steepled his hands in front of him. "Do you think Edward would approve a protection detail for her? Some loyalists were giving her a hard time."

She shrugged. "You can ask, but it seems unlikely." Abbie sipped her tea, then spit it out. "Ugh, I miss coffee. It's like a hug in a mug. This is . . . this is nothing but herb water." She dumped it down the sink and set the mug aside. "You must really like her if you're arranging for stocky men to protect her."

He shrugged one shoulder. "It can't go anywhere."

"Edward said something, I take it?"

Saint gave her a curt nod, and she shook her head sadly. "I'm sorry. I can't see him being okay with you dating a reporter as long as you're the communications officer. You know what a stickler he is for the rules. He's turned a blind eye to your hookups, but dating? I don't know. I don't see it happening." She got herself a glass of cold water. "Maybe if she wasn't covering the palace, but even then . . . if anything leaked, you know she'd be the one they'd blame. You don't want to put her in that situation."

"No. I don't." He slowly lowered his forehead to his arms. "But I can't get her out of my head."

"The sex is that good, huh?"

"We haven't had sex," he said without lifting his head. Abbie choked on her water, and Saint had to pat her on the back until she got her breath back.

"Are you sure you're not just fixated on what you can't have?"

"No, it's not just the forbidden fruit factor. I mean, yes, she's gorgeous. But she's got a kid—Olly, you met him when we played water balloon baseball. She's . . . cautious. Observant. She's different." He sighed. "She's great."

"A kid, huh? Do you like him, too?"

"I like most kids. Including this one. Even though he's a troublemaker."

"That's probably *why* you like him." She grinned at him over her glass. "I'll see what I can do. Maybe I can convince him somehow."

Saint blinked in surprise. "Thanks, Abbie. I'd really appreciate that."

"You got it, cowboy. Now go take those posters down, I've got stuff to do."

He chuckled. *You can take the title away from the royal, but you can't take the entitlement out of the royal.* "You got it, Grand Duchess," he teased, closing the doors behind him.

"Francis!"

CHAPTER TWENTY-THREE

THE RESTAURANT WAS crowded. Apparently, the masses wanted to eat fish and chips shaped like swords and spears near the holidays. Saint held the door for a group exiting the restaurant, then nudged the Everleighs inside. But they got caught in the doorway when another group seized the opportunity to leave.

"She's under the mistletoe," a passing woman said, smiling. He looked up. Brooke stood directly under it, but she hadn't heard the woman's comment. Saint tried not to panic; if she saw that she was under the mistletoe, he'd have to make a choice. He wasn't ready to kiss her and know that it was probably the first and last time, nor was he ready to see the hurt on her face when he rejected her.

"Walk," he barked at Brooke, and she glared at him incredulously over her shoulder before shuffling forward.

"I'm going to spend a penny," she said. "You two find a table."

He sighed with relief, rubbing the back of his neck, and herded Olly forward. She'd missed what the woman said, but Olly hadn't.

"It was mistletoe, Captain. You're supposed to kiss under mistletoe. It's bad luck if you don't. You have to."

"Who told you that? Uncle Judson, I suppose?"

"Yes. That's why he kissed her yesterday."

He did? He was too surprised to be angry.

"I can't, mate," Saint muttered. The wounded expression Olly gave him was like a fist to the gut.

"Don't you like Mum?"

He sat down at the next empty table so they were face-to-face. "Of course I like Mum, but I must honor her wishes. It's not just about what *I* want, is it?" *If I had my way, your mum and I would be back at my house, in front of the fire, a bottle of wine . . . and no kids.*

"She doesn't want you to kiss her?"

"No, she doesn't. She told me."

"When?"

"The first day we met." Saint smirked, remembering, as he spun his water glass.

Olly considered this. "Sometimes she changes her mind, you know . . ." Saint took a breath to respond, but Olly charged on. "Like if you want to watch *Karate Kats* and she says no, if you wait until she's on the phone and then ask again, she says yes. Maybe ask her again."

Saint chuckled and ruffled his hair. "It's complicated, mate . . . but I promise, it's not because I don't like her, all right? I like her a lot."

"What are you two whispering about?"

"Christmas secrets," Saint put in before Olly could say anything. "Highly classified. You should know better than to go around eavesdropping near the holiday." She raised an eyebrow but said nothing as Olly moved over and she slid into the booth. *Did she really kiss Judson, that ninny? Perhaps she's in love with him . . . Maybe I'm wasting my time here.*

He got the Castle Stormer, a double burger with everything on it, and she got a serf salad, the only vegetarian option on the menu. Lettuce that was more white than green, poorly shredded cheese, slimy tomatoes—he knew she'd only agreed to this restaurant for Olly's sake; she was always doing that, quietly sacrificing for him. It was high time someone did something for her. *I should take Olly shopping for Christmas. Maybe her mum's done it already, or Uncle Judson, the kiss-stealer. Still, what's the harm in one more present?*

Saint pulled out his phone while they were distracted by a discussion about whether it was appropriate to stab your chip into the ketchup while making screaming noises in a restaurant. (Spoiler alert: it wasn't.)

Saint: Have you taken Olly shopping for Brooke yet?

Boote: Shopping?

Saint: Christmas presents.

Boote: Presents, right. No, I haven't.

Saint: Mind if I do it?

Boote: Be my guest.

Saint: You realize it's in five days, right?

Boote: What I lack in punctuality, I make up for in sentimentality.

Saint: Macaroni picture frame, huh?

Boote: Funny.

Saint: Gee, isn't it bad luck not to get someone a present when they got you one?

Boote: No, it's just impolite, it's not bad luck.

Saint: You're the expert.

Boote: Olly told you I kissed her, didn't he?

Boote: Look, it was just a silly holiday thing. It was nothing.

Saint: Oh yeah?

Boote: She doesn't see me that way, never has. She's like a sister.

Saint: I've got a sister. Never kissed her under the mistletoe, though.

Boote: Don't hurt me.

"What are you scheming over there? Your look is severe."

"Work stuff."

That piqued her interest. "What work stuff?"

"Why do you care?"

She gave him half a smile. "Once a newshound, always a newshound," she said.

And that's exactly the problem, he thought. He turned to Olly. "What do you say you help me with a project tonight, mate? Top secret."

He nodded eagerly.

"That okay, Mum?"

She nodded. "Just not too late."

"Finish your dinner, then," Saint said.

"I am finished," he said, wiping his greasy hands on his coat.

"You've still got more than half your chicken nuggets left!"

Olly shrugged and Brooke smirked at him.

Saint leaned forward on his elbows. "How do you expect to grow up to be as big as me if you're not finishing your meals? War fighters need calories."

"I'm full," he whined, and Saint gave up.

"It's no wonder you're poor," he muttered as he took the bill up to the front.

"Captain," Brooke warned, giving him a hard look.

"Sorry, sorry. Let's go then. Kiss your mum goodbye."

Olly gave him a withering look at the mention of a kiss, and Saint didn't know if it was because he'd chickened out of kissing her under the mistletoe or because he had no desire to kiss his mum in public. He paid ($50 for *that*?) as Brooke packed up the leftovers, then ushered Olly out the front door.

"What's this project, then?"

"We're going to buy your mum some presents for Christmas. And don't bark at me, I already know you haven't got any money. We'll use my money, all right? Now what does she like?"

"She likes vegetables."

"No, mate—all right, that's my fault. She does like vegetables, you're right. But we want to spoil Mum, right? Let's get her something she wouldn't get for herself."

They boarded the train, Saint holding on to Olly's hood. Holding his hand felt a bit too paternal, but he didn't want to get separated. They found two seats near the front, and Olly turned to see out the window.

"So? What do you think?"

"About what?"

"Presents, Oliver. Presents for Mum." Good grief, is this why mums were always so sick of repeating themselves? The kid couldn't keep a request in his head for more than thirty seconds.

"Oh. Right." He looked out the window. "Hey, look at that big tree! Captain, did you see that big tree?"

"Yeah, I did see it," Saint muttered. *Right. Coming up with a gift is on me, apparently.*

"Let's get her video games." At least he was suggesting something . . .

"That's something you and I would like. But mums are different, eh? They don't like video games as much as we do."

"My mum does."

Saint rolled his eyes. "Really? What's her favorite, then?"

"What's that one with the shapes and you turn them to make them fit?"

"Brick Blockers?"

Old school. Is my girl an old-school gamer? Saint's brain tapped him on the shoulder to remind him she wasn't *his girl*, but he ignored it.

"Yes, Brick Blockers. She likes that one."

"Has she ever played Pirate's Cove?"

"What's it like?"

"It's a reading game—they give you choices and then you have to type in directions."

Olly rested his chin on the back of the seat. "I don't think we have that one, but I can't remember."

"All right, you can get her that one. The reading is pretty easy, you'd be able to play it too in a year or two."

"Great!" Olly grinned. "What are you going to get her?"

"Me?" Saint's mind went blank. Was he going to get her anything? "Did she get me something?"

Olly nodded.

"What'd she get?"

Olly gave him a disappointed look. "It's a secret."

"Oh, come on. Mum won't mind."

"Yes, she will. She made me promise not to tell."

Shit. Well, if she'd gotten him something, he had to reciprocate in kind.

"Well, let's start with yours and see how far we get." They got off the train at the mall. It was as busy as he'd feared; mostly, it was packed with people who didn't like to shop online.

"These old people are walking so sloooowwww," Olly complained loudly, and Saint shushed him as an elderly couple shot them annoyed glances over their shoulders.

But for once, a slow pace worked to his advantage. He looked around the mall as they continued their shuffle through the main channel, and there it was—his salvation—a day spa. *That's exactly what Everleigh deserves. And I can babysit. Perfect.*

Tugging on Olly's hood, he led them through the double glass doors of the quiet spa, which had a waterfall in the waiting area and tranquil piano music. Incense filled the room. Several very dyed, painted, coiffed ladies sat in chairs, reading magazines and using their phones. Before Olly could say anything, Saint turned to face him and crouched down.

"If you think it smells bad in here," he said softly, "or if you think it's boring, or if you hate the decor or the music, or any other comment you might have, you can keep that to yourself. Got it?"

The kid nodded, slightly sullen. He approached the desk and purchased a one-hundred-dollar gift card before Olly could embarrass them and they high-tailed it for the electronics store for the video game. Saint spotted a copy of Rabbit Crosses the Road, another old-school favorite, so he got that one, too. They had it paid for, wrapped up and ready in less than fifteen minutes. Of course, the amount of time that had passed was irrelevant to a five-year-old's stomach, and grumbling, Saint bought Olly a bag of popcorn. They were lucky they caught the train when they did: they squeezed through the crowd to claim the last two seats. Saint was absorbed in his phone and Olly in his snack when someone in front of them coughed.

He looked up. A very pregnant woman and her daughter were standing in front of him.

"Please, take our seats."

"What?" Olly protested. "How am I supposed to eat standing up?"

"Put your mind to work. I'm sure you'll come up with a creative solution."

The woman smiled gratefully as they traded places. Olly grabbed the pole, but his hands must've been slippery from the butter, because when the train's brakes slammed on at the next station, he went flying forward. Perhaps it was his years of military training, perhaps having an unnatural determination to protect, but Saint reached out for Olly's hood. Time, like the train, slowed quickly to a stop. He saw his own hand reaching, straining to grab the forest-green sweatshirt. He saw Olly's blond crew cut hurtling toward the ground, his head snap forward. For the briefest of moments, he could even see into the future: sitting in the emergency room with Olly, his broken nose spewing blood, Brooke reaming him out in front of the hospital staff, swearing he'd never be welcome at their home again. Perhaps it was that vision that propelled him just the tiniest bit faster and he hooked his fingers into the hood just in time to keep the boy from face-planting. He yanked back and caught Olly around the chest as the presents went sliding across the train.

"Are you okay? Are you all right?" Saint hugged Olly before he realized what he was doing, ran his fingers through the boy's hair, checking for blood or bumps, held him by the shoulders and looked him up and down, his heart imitating his drum solo on one of the band's more frantic numbers.

"Captain . . ." Olly gestured with his head toward a middle-aged black woman who was handing him the shopping bag he'd dropped. He took it and thanked her, still gripping Olly's hood like a lifeline.

In a small voice, Olly said, "Maybe you should hold my hand."

Saint sighed shakily. "Yeah, good call, mate." They held hands all the way back to Brooke's apartment, neither of them ready to let go, but he felt his anxiety growing with every step up to the fourth floor. "Perhaps we shouldn't . . ." Saint stopped himself. He wouldn't ask Olly to lie. It was just an accident; he'd protected the boy. Brooke would understand; he'd tell her himself.

He knocked on the front door and heard her call, "It's open!"

Scowling, he opened it. "Why is it open? You're a woman living alone for Woz's sake."

"I don't leave it open for His sake, I leave it open for mine." She grinned. "Hi, Oll. You have fun with the captain?"

The kid took a breath—and Woz love him, he looked to Saint for permission, as if he knew he'd put him in a bad light if he shared the scary part. He nodded.

Oliver turned back to Brooke, who had lifted one eyebrow. "He made me give up my seat on the train, and I almost fell, but he caught me. The rest was good, but it's a secret. Can I go take my shower?"

Brooke looked confused, her eyes bouncing between them as she paused her knitting. "Sure, bud. Call me if you want help with your hair." Watching him go, Saint trudged over to the couch and sat down hard next to her. He put his head in his hands, resting his elbows on his knees.

"All right, let me have it."

"My dishcloth? You can't, it's not done yet."

"No," he said, impatient. "Tell me I can't take him out again, tell me I should've paid better attention. Yell at me. Get it over with."

"I am so genuinely perplexed right now, I couldn't begin to explain it." She scratched his back lightly with her fingernails, and he felt his muscles go limp. "Was Olly hurt?"

"No. But he almost—"

Brooke laughed. "Captain, do you know how many times a day Olly *almost* hurts himself? Or *actually* hurts himself? I'm more careful with him than anyone, and he still comes up with new bumps and bruises daily."

He raked his fingers over his scalp. "This would've been bad, this would've been so bad. There would've been blood everywhere. I shouldn't have made him get up, but the pregnant lady needed the seat . . ."

"Captain, look at me."

He couldn't, he couldn't bear to see disappointment on her face. *Am I turning into Sam now? What is happening to me?*

"Saint." Her voice, so sweet, so soft, drew him out of his worst-case-scenario imaginings. "Olly's okay. You're okay. That's what matters. I know you're careful with him. It's okay."

He looked up, and she swept the hair off his forehead. Saint felt himself stiffen; it wasn't the actual touch, it was the trust in it. He wanted to lean into that, yet there was something else. Like she knew touching him wasn't going to lead anywhere romantic. How could she be so comfortable touching him when every brush of her fingers made him feel electrified? He grabbed her wrist.

"I'm not Judson. Don't patronize me."

"I'm not patronizing you, I'm comforting you." She lowered her voice to a whisper. "And you're hurting my arm." He let her go immediately, rubbing his hands on his jeans, guilt swamping his thoughts.

"Shit, I'm sorry. Are you okay? Do you need ice?" He shot off the couch and went to the freezer, looking for that frozen penguin ice pack, shifting around the ground beef and bagged mixed vegetables, searching. He hadn't found it yet when he felt Brooke's arms wrapping around him from behind, holding him tight, her cheek resting between his shoulder blades.

"It's scary, isn't it? When they almost get hurt?"

Saint exhaled hard, letting the warm air of his breath condensate in the cold air of the freezer, since he was still holding the door open. He didn't trust his voice; emotion clogged his throat, from the combination of her sincere lack of anger, her warm embrace, and her bull's-eye assessment of his feelings. He tried again to clear his throat when Olly's voice came down the hall.

"Is Captain Saint still here? Can he read my story?"

"See?" Brooke whispered, letting him go. "Olly still trusts you, too." She came around to look into his eyes, and he made a mental note that the military should weaponize her eye color, because it was the most disarming shade of blue he'd ever encountered. "Do you want to read to him?"

"Sure." He cleared his throat again—that damn lump just wouldn't go away. Saint strode down the hall toward Olly's room and found him already in bed with a pensive expression clouding his face.

"Was she mad?" he whispered.

"No, mate. She said you fall down all the time." He forced a grin to reassure the boy, and Olly grinned back. Saint read him a book about an elf who saved Christmas. After, Olly went and brushed his teeth, then got up again for a drink of water, then to find his bear. When Saint finally tucked the quilt around him, Olly was yawning. He felt tense again about the physical contact and had preemptively decided on a good-night fist bump—until Olly threw his arms around his neck. Dropping to one knee, he gave the boy a firm hug and felt his heart melt like a candy cane left on the radiator. Olly turned his head to rest it on his shoulder, and Saint felt that damn lump coming back. He coughed and turned to see Brooke standing in the doorway, waiting her turn. She put a hand on his arm as he edged past her back into the hall.

"Don't leave yet, okay?"

How had she known he was going to try to sneak out? *Too smart for her own good . . . and possibly mine.* He took the opportunity to put her presents under the Christmas tree, pitiful though it was. He was standing by the front door with his coat and shoes on when she came back.

"Off so soon? I bought beer, some kind of holiday blend. Pine something."

His heart constricted painfully. *For me. She bought beer because she wants me to hang out here with her, even though she has no income . . .*

"You shouldn't have, I can't stay. See you later." He had his hand on the doorknob when he felt her hand on his arm.

"Wait a minute. Just slow down, would you?" He wished she'd stop touching him. Paired with her tender concern, his control over his emotions was getting more slippery than the penguin ice pack he never found.

"What's wrong?"

"Nothing. I'm fine, Everleigh. Everything's fine."

"Now who's being patronizing?"

"I don't do feelings talk. Quit trying to back me into a corner."

"Look, you're obviously upset about what happened on the train . . ."

"If you keep pushing me, you won't like what happens next."

She crossed her arms. "Stop trying to scare me. It's not working."

"I'm not trying to scare you," he said through gritted teeth. "I'm trying to warn you before we both say and do things we shouldn't."

She held her arms out wide, raising her voice. "Say whatever you want. Do whatever you want. Just don't shut me out!"

He turned toward the door. "I'm leaving."

She followed, cutting him off. "I can take whatever you can dish out, Captain. I've never run from a fight in my life. Where do you think my kid gets it?" Her eyes were blazing, her posture rigid as a post; she was bouncing on her toes, her fists balled at her sides like she wanted to punch him. "You're a damn coward."

Saint charged her, backing her up into the front door. "I'm not jacking scared. I just don't. Do. Feelings. Talk."

"Why the Jersey not?"

"Because no one wants to hear it!" he roared, slamming his open palm against the door above her head.

"Maybe I do!" she shouted back, lifting her chin defiantly. "Maybe I care about you! Maybe I hate seeing you in pain!"

"Bullshit, Everleigh! We're friends, *just friends*, because that's how *you* wanted it."

"Maybe I wouldn't want it that way if you weren't an emotionally unavailable jackass who flirts with anything in a skirt!"

Don't bite. Don't take that bait.

"I haven't seen anyone else in months, and you know it," he shouted back. "Bottom line: you don't have the right to demand *anything*. You don't have the right to extort my feelings out of me. You're not my girlfriend; you're not my wife. So you can care all you want, but it doesn't mean jack."

"Fine. Hide behind labels. Put up your impenetrable man wall of numbness and denial. But no matter what you tell yourself, you're not protecting yourself. You're hurting yourself, and you're hurting us, too. And if that's how it's going to be, then I'm glad we're moving."

Brooke paled, and he felt as if someone had thrown open the window to let the winter weather freeze him on the spot. "You're moving? Where?"

She stared at him, hands over her mouth, silent for once.

"To West Cheekton, or what?" he prompted.

She shook her head, slowly. *Farther?*

"Radishcliff? Quarryville? Troutbluff?" It would take him all day to get out there and back, but it was doable on weekends. Maybe he could crash with a friend so he didn't have to do both directions on the same day. Crashing with her was a bad idea . . . for a variety of reasons.

"We're going to Gardenia with my mum. Charlie won't be able to sue for custody of Olly across kingdom lines. I've got a job lined up as a restaurant reviewer."

Saint's mouth went dry. *What? Gardenia? That's the opposite side of the continent.* He turned away to lean with both hands against the wall, his chin dropping. *This isn't happening. I need time to convince her, I need more time with both of them, I need . . . them.*

He kept his voice low. "When?"

"Just after New Year's."

Getting himself together, he straightened, crossing his arms over his chest. "Never run from a fight, huh? Sure feels like that's what's happening here."

Her eyes turned hard. "No one's going to take my son. You have no idea what it's like to think you might lose someone who's your whole life."

Except you just said you're moving . . . so now I do. He put his hand on the doorknob again, and she covered it with hers, then quickly removed it and stepped aside when he gave her a taste of the turmoil he was feeling in his gaze.

Brooke was wringing her hands, her eyes softer now. "Saint, don't. Don't just storm off; let's talk about this. I shouldn't have sprung it on you like that. I'm sorry. Please, let's just discuss this . . ."

"Sounds like the decision is already made. I don't see what's to discuss." Saint put his mask of detachment back in place; he didn't want her sympathy. He just needed to make it out onto the street, and then he could explode. Good thing for his neighbors he had headphones for his drum set at home.

"It's not personal," she whispered. "We just—"

"Are we still on for Christmas?"

She opened her mouth, then shut it again. Brooke nodded, her eyes on the floor.

"Then I'll see you then. Text me when you're up."

"Okay," she whispered, and he could hear the tears clogging her throat. If he didn't leave now, there was no way he could hold back the torrent that was building inside him. He lunged for the door again, and this time, she didn't stop him.

CHAPTER TWENTY-FOUR

SAINT: What are you doing?

Brooke: Just cleaning up from dinner.

Saint: Come over.

Brooke: What, now? It's late.

Saint: It's only 6:30.

Brooke: But it's dark out.

Saint: It's winter. It's dark at 4:30.

Saint: Please? I need to talk to you.

Brooke: It's almost Olly's bedtime.

Saint: I know. I asked Judson to sit with him so we could talk.

Saint: He's on his way over now.

Brooke: Why can't you come here?

Saint: Reasons.

Saint: Please?

Saint: Hire a wagon.

Brooke huffed a humorless laugh. Saint, ever the man in charge. *What if I'd had plans?* Her only plans probably would've been with Judson, and if he was free, Saint probably figured she was, too. Besides, she didn't go out on weeknights. Or weekends . . .

Brooke: That was overstepping, by the way, to ask Judson.

Brooke: But I'll be over as soon as Olly's in bed.

She decided to walk, even though it was cold out. She'd spent too much on presents for Olly, even though she'd promised herself that she wouldn't this year. Brooke was tired of saying no. At the grocery store checkout line, when he asked for candy. For the after-school martial arts class. When he wanted to go out to eat instead of making something cheap at home. The guilt about moving him away from his few friends, even though those friends were mostly adult men and various dogs, had been weighing heavily on her when she clicked "Buy" on that new tablet. She wished now she'd thought it through more and gotten him a new bike . . . but she'd have had to find time to put it together before Christmas. Of course, it was just going to be harder to move once it was assembled, and the roads would've been icy anyway. She was thinking about whether she should return the tablet when she turned onto Saint's street. Brooke could see him pacing, his hulking shadow sliding across the closed curtains. His Christmas tree was lit, its uniform white lights glowing softly.

She smiled at the sight, then her chest immediately felt tight. *Sugar, I'm going to miss him so much.* Her gut told her that he'd asked her here to talk her out of moving or yell at her more about how he hated feelings, but her traitorous heart saw that pacing shadow and wondered . . . *wanted* more from him. *It would be the best Christmas present ever.* Brooke internally crushed that line of thinking as she came up the walk to his house stomping the snow from her boots.

At the sound, he peeked out the front curtains and threw open the front door. "Where the Jersey have you been? You said you were coming right over! I called you ten times!"

Brooke patted her pockets. "Oh, I must've left my phone at home." *No wonder my walk was so peaceful. I hope Judd doesn't need anything.*

"And you *walked*? Just walking through the city at night with no phone in the snow?"

"I had my bear spray."

He threw his arms up in the air, clearly exasperated. "Just, just . . . walking alone?"

Brooke grinned up at him. "It's quite cold. May I come in before you continue your harangue?"

His eyes narrowed. "My harangue?"

"Yes, you know," she said, wiping her boots carefully on the mat. "*Harangue, a noun. A lengthy and aggressive speech.* Synonyms include *rant, diatribe, tirade, lecture, homily, berating*—"

"I'm not berating you." His eyes softened as he moved aside so she could come in, where she unwrapped her scarf, took off her hat, and, with Saint's help, shrugged out of her coat. She slipped off her shoes before he could ask. His house was nice and warm, but she shivered a little. *Alone with Saint in his house. Funny, I feel far more unsafe here than I did out on the street . . . Maybe I should've left the coat on, in case I need to make a quick getaway.* Christmas music was playing over the stereo, a woman singing a slow song with a jazz trio about togetherness and making it a holiday to remember and hope for the next year; Brooke tried not to read too much into it. There was a fire in the fireplace, red-and-white peppermint candles lit on the coffee table and kitchen table, nestled in evergreen wreaths . . . It felt so warm and homey. So like him to make visitors feel comfortable. Buster lifted his head from his bed and thumped his tail at the sight of her.

"Do you want tea? Cocoa?"

"That depends," she said, rubbing her hands together, trying to warm them with the friction. "How long is this haranguing going to take?" She looked up at her friend, and now that she was inside where the light was better, she could see the dark circles under his eyes, the slump of his shoulders. Brooke moved closer to him instinctively. "What's wrong?"

"Nothing." He flinched when she touched his biceps, and she knew it wasn't just because her hands were freezing. She pulled back hesitantly, dropping her gaze.

"I'll take peppermint tea, if you have it."

To her surprise, he turned and retrieved a steaming mug from the kitchen counter. "Here."

"You already made it? How'd you know what I'd want?"

"I just . . . I just made one of everything. I'll drink whatever you don't want." She looked and noticed the steaming pot of cocoa, a skin forming on the surface, and three more cups of tea, which she assumed were different varieties.

"Are you okay?"

"Of course. Here, sit down." He pointed her toward the couch.

Right. Of course. He doesn't do feelings.

She sipped her tea and turned toward him on the brown leather sofa. "So what was so urgent?"

"I want to know what I can get Olly for the holiday."

She shrugged. "Whatever you want."

Saint still looked very tense, and she thought about offering him a foot rub. That always put her at ease. "Whatever I want?" he echoed. "No, I need better information than that. I don't want to upstage whatever you have planned."

Brooke smiled. "That's very considerate, but I kind of overspent, so I doubt that'll happen. I got him a new tablet. Well, it's new to him, anyway."

He nodded, rubbing at his chin; it had a few days' stubble. *That isn't like him.* This wasn't adding up, any of it. He could've texted all this. She put down her tea and scooted closer to him, leaving about an inch of space between their legs. He stood up immediately, rubbing his hands on his jeans.

"I'm sorry," he muttered. "I don't know why I asked you over. I . . . I've wasted your time. I'm sorry."

Her stomach clenched watching him struggle. *I don't know how to put him at ease again, help him find the words he can't seem to get out. Not that my efforts worked so well the last time we were together . . .*

"Okay. I understand." She sat back against the leather couch cushions.

He stilled. "You do?"

"Sure," she said, shrugging one shoulder, leaning over to retrieve her tea. "Honesty is hard. Maybe you'll tell me next time, whatever it is." She smiled in a way she hoped was reassuring. He rubbed the back of his neck, his face going pink in an adorable way.

"Will you dance with me?"

Brooke felt her lips part as they opened in shock. "Dance with you?"

He nodded. "I think it'll help."

"Help how?" she asked, and she knew that her sincere confusion was coming through in her smile just fine, based on the embarrassed look on his face. He just held out his hand, and she accepted it and stood up into his arms. Brooke, being shorter than he was, turned her head to rest her ear against his chest and wrapped her arms around his middle. The pounding of his heart eventually slowed, his shoulders dropped, and he let out a big sigh. She felt his fingers combing the ends of her long hair, then he stopped and just held her around her shoulders. Their feet moved together, a slow rhythm that was more shuffle than step.

"I want to tell you a story, and I just want you to listen. Two stories. And they might not seem to go together, and you might not want to hear them, but just listen until I'm done, and then you can go, okay?"

She nodded, her cheek rubbing his firm chest. *Gah . . . that chest.* She forced herself not to turn her head and give it a little kiss. It deserved so much more. So did the heart inside it.

"I grew up without a dad, for a long time. I know you did, too. But for a man, I think it's different. You don't know how to be a man unless someone shows you. My dad—my adopted dad—he spent time with me. A lot of time. More than the other kids, and I knew it, but I didn't even feel guilty, I ate it up. I was so hungry for a man to care about me. I needed it more, I had a lot of catch-up to do. And I can't tell you what to do, because I don't know Charlie . . ." She stiffened at Olly's dad's name; this was not at all where she thought this conversation was going, but it certainly explained why he'd been so nervous. He rubbed her back in big, slow circles until she relaxed again.

"I don't know Charlie," he repeated, "but I know Oliver. And he's great, he's so great. And if he was my son . . ." Saint coughed to clear his throat. "I'd want him in my life, too. I know it would be hard to share him, so hard. But you're strong. You're so much tougher than you give yourself credit for. So even though you're moving, I think you should consider giving Charlie a chance to be a dad, especially since he won't have me and Judson around anymore."

Brooke squeezed him briefly. "Okay." His care for Olly touched her heart. His perspective on the situation was unique, and she appreciated that he'd share it with her, even though it was obviously painful for him and he seemed to worry that she'd be upset. "What's the other story?"

He cleared his throat again and his fingers went back to combing her hair. "There was just one story."

"No," she whispered. "You said there were two. I want both. I want to know what's going on in your head, in your heart."

"You're remembering wrong."

"No. Tell me."

He swore like only a military man could and held her tighter, like he was afraid she was going to bolt. "Fine, but remember: you asked for this."

"I take full responsibility." Even though her stomach was coughing up acid into her throat, and emotions were making it hard to breathe, she had to hear it. She had to know what he wanted to say, just in case it was what she needed to hear.

"You were going into that ridiculous restaurant, the medieval one, and you were under the mistletoe, but you didn't see it." Cheeks burning, Brooke tried to lift her head to see him better, but he gently pressed it back against his chest. "But I saw it, and Olly did, too. He told me it was bad luck that I didn't kiss you. And I know I have to let you go to Gardenia, because that's what you want. But before you go, just to reverse the bad luck I gave you, I just wanted to see if you'd . . ." He shifted to pull something out of his pocket and let her go enough that she could see the mistletoe he held over her head on a thin red ribbon. "I just wanted to make sure you'll have good luck before you go."

He wants to kiss me goodbye.

"Okay." She nodded, trying not to look too eager.

"Just to clarify," he said, bringing his other hand to the back of her neck, "I don't want the kind of kiss you gave Judson." He was not smiling. *Not. At. All.* In fact, he was almost pouting, his pink lower lip protruding even more than usual. *Jealous much, Captain?*

A nervous laugh bubbled out of her chest. "That? That was nothing."

"Which is why I don't want that kind." He shifted even closer to her, all earnest-eyed, his left foot coming between hers, and she figured this was about as close to a declaration of love as she was ever going to get from this tight-lipped bastard. She nodded, schooling her face into solemnity.

"So, just to clarify, you want a kiss that's *something*?"

"Yes."

"What sort of something?"

She expected annoyance at her teasing, but he stayed sincere. "A sweet something. Not like you kissed me when you were drunk." His thumb lightly stroked her cheek.

She smiled. "How did I kiss you when I was drunk?"

"Hungry."

"Hi—have you seen yourself? You can hardly blame me. It's been a long five years . . ."

He looked into the fire, shaking his head, scowling. "This is coming out wrong. This isn't—"

"Saint."

He looked back at her with clear trepidation.

"It's coming out fine. Now I'm going to give you a sweet something kiss that's entirely for the benefit of my good luck."

Saint lifted one eyebrow. "For the luck to work, I think *I'm* supposed to give it to *you* . . ."

"I'll risk it," she said, pulling him down to touch that pouty lip to hers. She kissed him slowly, pressing him firmly against her everywhere she could reach, and he sighed out through his nose like he'd been holding his breath. After a few moments, Brooke upped the ante, sliding her tongue shyly along the seam of his lips, and he opened for her immediately. *Apparently, using my tongue does not make it too hungry.* His tongue touched hers in tiny tastes, and she could taste the cocoa he must've had before she got there. Saint tossed aside the mistletoe, and his hands slid down to her backside to lift her up so their faces were level. *That's better.* Brooke wrapped her legs around his waist, cinching herself around him like a belt, still kissing him slowly, languidly, like she never had to leave and never wanted to. With half an ear, she listened with delight to the fire crackle and the jazz singer croon, asking what the object of her affection was doing New Year's Eve. *New Year's. I'm leaving after New Year's.* Her stomachache was back, even as her skin flushed under his touch.

"Saint," she murmured, feeling every finger of his hands on her backside. "What are we doing?"

"Kissing," he answered. Though he didn't say it, she heard the *"finally"* in his tone. He turned and sat them on the couch, not giving her any room to shy away, his hands coming up immediately to tangle in her long hair and cradle her neck.

Brooke decided to ignore her mind's objections that this was *Foolish with a capital F* and let her body have its way for once. She did not allow her heart to weigh in, though she had a sneaking suspicion which bits of her it would side with. Brooke leaned into his gentle caresses, enjoying the long, loose feeling of her whole body. She wasn't a rational person now, she'd melted and re-formed into a creature of instinct and impulse, wholly focused on the sensation of being close to Saint, this grumpy-but-secretly-sensitive man she respected and trusted . . . and loved.

Damn it, heart, I told you to keep quiet. Go to time-out.

"I'm going to walk you home now," he whispered, breaking the kiss to bring their foreheads together.

"Already? I could stay a little longer . . ." *Yes, my body is clearly calling the shots.*

He shook his head, even as he pressed light kisses onto her cheeks and neck. "If you do, there'll be a different kind of luck happening, and it'll be a lot more mutual."

"I see," she said. *Would that be so bad?* Her brain protested loudly at this line of thinking, citing even the remote possibility of another baby she couldn't afford as ample reason to let the man walk her home.

Saint interrupted her thoughts. "Thank you for letting me right my wrong."

"Oh, it was my pleasure," she replied, her voice sounding huskier than normal.

He groaned, kissing her lips again. "Don't use that voice."

"What voice?"

"Your sex voice."

She laughed low. "My sex voice? How would you know what my sex voice sounds like?"

"Because it's exactly how I've imagined it for months, you vixen."

He has? Um, what? He pushed gently on her hips to get her to stand up. Brooke picked up her teacup; it was stone cold. *How long have I been here?* She took it to the kitchen and dumped the liquid down the drain. Her heart went with it; there would be no more of this. No more sweet Sundays, no more snowball fights. No more the three of them going out to eat or for a walk. No more toe-curling, heart-melting kisses.

She felt herself tearing up, and she kept her back to him to try to hide it. But her running nose betrayed her.

"Brooke?"

She swiped at her eyes, still giving him her back. "What?"

"You okay?"

"Of course."

Saint pressed in behind her and turned her, scowling. "Hiding feelings is my thing, not yours. Stay in your own lane, woman."

"I don't know why I'm crying."

"Really? I do. And I'm 'an emotionally unavailable jackass,' even though I've stopped looking at anyone else's skirts . . . ," he said. She laughed, but he went on. "Just like I know why you're really leaving."

Guilt stabbed at her. Charlie was part of it; she didn't want to share Olly. She didn't want Charlie screwing him up somehow, hurting his feelings, upsetting the delicacy of the good place they'd been in lately. But that wasn't all of it. She hadn't even admitted to herself that she was running from Saint.

"I want to go home now."

He stared down at her, clearly torn. Then he turned and retrieved her coat and held it for her while she put her arms in the sleeves. He followed her all the way home, as silent tears turned to icy trails on her cheeks. He paused on the top step of the stairway, hands shoved in his pockets, his feet in a wide stance, just watching her.

"Good night. Thank you for . . . for the luck. I have a feeling I'll need it."

He didn't say anything, but he kept staring at her. She closed the door, locked it, and rested her head against it.

"Hey!"

Brooke jumped; she'd forgotten Judson was there. "You scared me!"

"Sorry. Everything all right?"

She didn't bother taking off her winter gear. She sat down on the couch next to him and leaned her head onto his shoulder. "The second-worst feeling I know is wanting to do the right thing and not having a darn clue what that is."

"What's the first-worst?"

"Thinking you knew the right thing, then finding out you were so, so wrong." She wiped her face. "Am I doing the right thing in moving across the continent? Should I give Charlie a chance? I honestly have no idea."

He patted her leg awkwardly. "I don't know, love."

"I'm so lost, Judson. I know it was the right thing for Mom to move back home and take care of Grandma, but it devastated me. The right thing for me is to be near her; she's the only close family I have. But I don't want to ruin Olly's life, ripping him away from you and Saint and his dad, away from his school and his friends. What do you do when you can't make everyone happy? When not everyone can have what they need? When every combination is literally, heartbreakingly impossible?" He started to answer, but she interrupted him. "How can I stay? I know myself; it's amazing I've stayed away from him this long. And if we do start a relationship, I know he'd resign. He's worked so hard for this, Judd—you have no idea. But I still need to work to support my kid, and journalism is what I'm qualified for. Even if I wasn't covering the palace, if any sensitive information was leaked, they'd blame me. In Edward's eyes, I'll always be the enemy."

"Couldn't you quit? Let him support you?"

She sniffled. "That's putting too much pressure on a relationship that's not really a relationship yet. Anyway, I don't think it would help." She wiped her running nose on her sleeve, not caring anymore.

"Did you ever read those Choose-Your-Own-Escapade books as a kid?" he asked.

"What?" Sometimes Judson was so obtuse, she just wanted to slap him into next week.

"Remember? They say, 'If you want to attack the octopus, turn to page 37. If you want to swim away, turn to page 94.'"

"What about it?"

"I think life is more like that than we realize. You think you're choosing your own escapade, your own path, but more often than not, you end up in the same place you would've anyway."

"Are you saying I'll end up with Saint anyway if I leave?"

"Perhaps. If it's meant to be."

"You know I don't believe in fate."

"It's all right; you don't have to. It still exists."

She considered this quietly for a few long moments before she sighed. "Thanks."

"Anytime."

AT 2 A.M., SHE GAVE up on sleep and grabbed her phone off the nightstand.

Brooke: We can't be together.

She didn't have to wait long for an answer; she didn't think he'd been asleep, either.

Saint: Why?

Brooke: You know why. You'd ruin your career.

Brooke: I'm not doing that to you.

Saint: Edward would get over it.

Brooke: I don't think that's true, babe . . .

The pet name just slipped out, as easy as breathing. She'd been using it in her head for weeks now, and she should've known it was inviting trouble. She should've erased it. She shouldn't have hit "Send."

Saint: Babe, if we're working out nicknames, you should've warned me.

Saint: I've got a whole list prepared for you, blondie.

Brooke: Did you want me to stay?

There was a long pause.

Saint: Did I want you to spend the night with me tonight?

No, she thought, laughing to herself, *pretty sure I know the answer to that.*

Brooke: No, stay in Orangiers. Not move. Stay and try to . . . relationship.

Her brain was mushy. She was no longer wired to enjoy nighttime activities . . . with a few specific exceptions. Wisely, he did not razz her about her verbal flub.

Saint: Of course I do.

Brooke dialed his number, burrowing deeper under the covers, as if they were a refuge from the hard conversation that was coming.

"Hi, babe."

Talk about sex voice. Gah.

"You say 'of course' like it's a given, Saint. I have no idea what's happening in your head. Until you kissed me, I wasn't even 100 percent sure you thought about me that way; you brushed me off so easily when I came on to you when I was drunk. I didn't think—"

He snorted. "Easily? Are we recalling the same event?"

"Given all that's happened between us . . ." She shook her head. "You have to start giving me more to work with if you want me to understand you."

"Babe, you painted me as this horrible skirt-chasing manslut before we even met. You'd already decided who I was, and you wrote me off—*permanently*. I think I was entitled to a little information from you, too, if you changed your mind . . ."

"Wasn't hanging out with you every weekend enough information?"

"It could be for Olly's benefit . . ."

"No, it couldn't."

"I wanted to think otherwise," he said softly, "but I wasn't sure."

"Why didn't you ask me?"

"You told me *never*, Everleigh. Those were my orders."

"I'm not your CO."

He snorted. "You clearly don't realize the sway you hold over me, beautiful."

Brooke was quiet. Trying to absorb this new information into her tired brain was like doing calculus with finger paint. It would probably work . . . but it was messy. "I have a lot to think about," she said quietly. "I'm not promising anything."

"I wouldn't ask you to." He paused. "Will you come with me to the palace New Year's Eve party, though? As my date? Please?"

"Yes." She was glad he wasn't there to see her embarrassingly large grin, but based on his low chuckle, he could hear it anyway. "Sweet dreams, Saint."

"You too, love."

CHAPTER TWENTY-FIVE

THROUGH THE FOG OF heavy sleep, Saint heard his phone buzz. Then it buzzed again. And again. He groped for it, but he couldn't reach it without getting out of bed. That had been intentional, knowing it might be early when Brooke texted, and he didn't want to be tempted to go back to sleep afterwards.

Brooke: HAPPY CHRISTMAS, FRANCIS DANIEL SAINT

Brooke: The Everleighs are UP

The next text was a selfie of Brooke and Olly in matching pajamas, smiling so wide the gap between his lower front teeth showed. His heart swelled, and he tapped the photo to save it. He hoped she didn't get dressed—he wanted to snuggle with her in those soft flannel pajama pants. Saint groaned and covered his head with the pillow. He was so in love with her, even when she was being insane. She was going to leave and take his heart with her, and now he had to go put on a happy face for Olly's sake. That was a lot to ask at 6:35 a.m.

Brooke: Come hungry. We have festive coffee and treats.

Saint: What is a festive treat?

Saint: Or is only the coffee festive?

Brooke: Come over and see.

Saint: So. Early.

Brooke: You were warned. My holiday spirit cannot be contended with.

Brooke: It has no decency when it comes to time.

Saint: Okay.

Brooke: ARE YOU COMING OR NOT

Saint: Woman. No yelling.

Saint: Getting dressed now.

Brooke: HURRY. STOCKINGS WAIT FOR NO MAN.

Saint rolled out of bed and pulled his academy sweatshirt off the end of the footboard. He checked his email for palace emergencies while the coffee brewed and Buster did a morning backyard sniff. The passenger load on the train was light, given the early hour and its darkness except for Christmas trees all lit up in everyone's windows. He trudged up the steps, feeling every one; it was possible he'd overdone it on his workout after he'd kissed her a few nights ago. He'd figured excessive exercise and a cold shower was the only way he'd sleep. It hadn't helped.

She threw open the front door before he could even knock.

"What took you so long?!" she cried, and he put a hand over her mouth.

"Your holiday enthusiasm is going to wake the neighbors, love." Both hands on the doorjamb, she was barring his way into the apartment, and he had a moment's confusion . . . until she glanced pointedly upward. *Mistletoe. Don't remember that being there a few days ago . . .* It was very good that she was holding on to him, because his knees immediately went a little weak and he felt his cheeks flush, fighting the redness the cold had wrought. Moving his hand to her waist, he kissed her slowly, savoring her warm against his cold.

"When did I tell you my middle name?" he asked, pretending to be stern.

"You never did. It was in the background check I ran on you when you started meeting with Olly as his mentor. I've had it in my back pocket all this time for when I needed to get your attention."

"That's such a mum thing to do." He kissed her again.

"Which part?"

"All of it." He kissed her longer this time; he'd opened the floodgates now.

"Whatever. You love it."

"Do you hear me denying it?" *I'm allowed to kiss Brooke Everleigh.* He already felt wired, like he'd had too much sugar, and the holiday hadn't even really started. She moved so he could come in, and he saw Olly coming down the hall. "Hey, happy Christmas, mate."

"Captain! Finally!" The boy dragged him over to the couch, as Brooke tried to help him out of his coat.

"Just a minute, just a minute, Oliver," he chuckled. Brooke took his layers and hung them up as he surveyed the room. She had Christmas music playing through the speakers via her phone, a fireplace on the TV, three fuzzy red-and-white stockings hung from the entertainment center. They were packed to the brim with small tissue-wrapped gifts, including one with his name on it. It was on a piece of masking tape, and it had obviously been put there by Oliver, but it was there.

The Everleighs were both buzzing around like they'd had six cups of coffee, and he just sat on the couch and let them wear themselves out. Eventually, they settled down enough to open gifts.

"So, did you buy stocking gifts for yourself?"

She nodded. "But some my mom sent."

Olly's stocking contained art supplies, sidewalk chalk, a few little cars and gadgety things, a chocolate orange. And then, because it was Brooke, there was also a new toothbrush, toothpaste, and three pairs of socks she'd knit. Her own stocking mainly contained gourmet food items: jars of roasted garlic and artichokes, pine nuts, vanilla. Seeing what she considered a luxury made him doubly glad he'd sprung for the spa gift card.

Saint was enjoying watching them coo and gasp over each silly thing, but they eventually noticed that he hadn't touched his own gifts.

"Go on then," Brooke said, getting up for more coffee that he thought she really didn't need. Hesitantly, he opened the first small present. He rattled the white box, and Olly giggled excitedly.

"What's this one?"

"Open it!"

Saint opened the cardboard box, only to find twelve bone-shaped cookies. "For Buster?"

Olly nodded, literally bouncing on the couch. "Mum and I found a recipe on the internet!" He was touched that they'd thought about his dog. The other things were small . . . His favorite candy bar. A pack of sanitizing wipes for meet and greets. A book of pictures Olly had drawn, some of which were really good. Those were going right onto his fridge. *Why? So you can miss them every time you eat?* He pushed the punishing voice away. He felt disappointed when he reached the bottom of his stocking . . . He'd secretly hoped for something made by her, too.

Brooke rubbed her hands together. "Do you need a bathroom break before we dive into real presents?"

He shook his head. "I know it's fascinating to you, Everleigh, but stop asking questions about my body. I'm capable of regulating it myself."

"Fine, but no breaks until all the presents are open."

"Fine." He got up and rummaged around the tree until he found one with his name on it. Saint shook it, but it didn't make any sound. "Not a book."

"No . . ."

Olly giggled, and Brooke gave him a quelling look.

"It better not be anything weird."

"Weird?" Her face was placidly neutral, but she hid behind her coffee cup.

"Yes, Everleigh. Weird. It better not bite, burn, or otherwise injure me."

"I can't believe you think me capable of such a thing . . ."

He glared at her as he ripped into the present, then stopped suddenly. In a navy blue that perfectly complemented his coat, she'd knitted him a hat with two thin white stripes, a pair of matching mittens, and a scarf.

"It's all wool," she said. "None of that synthetic stuff. It should keep you very warm."

He didn't know what to say, so he stared at the pieces, fingering their rough weave. Neither Calynda nor his mum was much into making things unless it was food. He'd never been doted upon like this before, and it felt . . . good. Strange, but good. Emotion welled in his chest.

"You know, perhaps I will use the facilities . . ."

"Try them on," she prompted gently.

"Yeah, try them on!" Olly yelled. "Took her flippin' forever to get the mittens right. She had to start over like ten times."

"Language," Brooke chided, her cheeks dusted with pink. Her eyes met his, and he saw her vulnerability; she hadn't spent much money on the gift, but she'd been thoughtful. Still, she seemed uncertain whether it was enough. He fitted the hat onto his head, then wound the long scarf around his neck and pulled on the mittens. He stood up, grinning down at her, and turned so that she could see him from a variety of angles.

Brooke nodded approvingly. He was never going to take them off. Saint moved to the Christmas tree again to find his gift to her. It hardly seemed like enough now. Maybe he should've done two hundred dollars. Olly beat him to it, finding one for himself.

"Olly, I need to talk to you before you open that one," Brooke said. "You got one bigger present instead of a bunch of little ones this year . . ." The boy, who had already ripped off the paper, stared slack-jawed at the box.

"A TABLET?" he shouted, and she nodded, grinning.

"Say thank you," Saint prompted, but Olly ignored him in favor of ripping the box open.

"I already charged it," Brooke said, as he tried to frantically get the box open. "Slow down now, please."

"Well, we've lost his attention for the rest of the day," Saint chuckled, handing her his present.

She ripped it open with as much gusto as Olly had his. "The day spa? Seriously?" She looked delighted, shocked.

"You like it?"

She beamed, bouncing her eyebrows. "I love it, I'm just surprised you'd want another man's hands on me, that's all."

He felt his face harden. "What are you talking about?"

"The massage artists there are all men . . . big hands . . . big, strong hands. Those guys are gonna work my kinks right out."

He plucked the slip of paper out of her hands. "Changed my mind."

"Saint!" She reached for it, but he held it away.

"And please, don't say 'kinks' in polite company."

"That's my present!" She reached across his lap, but she was still too short to reach.

"I'll get you something safer, like a book."

"Books have never been safe. They contain every kind of dangerous idea about how life ought to be." She held her hand out flat, and, disgruntled, he put the gift certificate back into her possession. "Oh," she cooed, "for that amount, I can get the full body instead of just neck and shoulders . . ."

"Vixen. Stop it."

Brooke giggled.

"What's a vixen?" Olly asked, not looking up from the tablet.

"Of course that's the one thing you hear, little man." Saint leaned over to see what he was doing. "Did Mum download you anything fun?"

"Learning your letters *is* fun," Brooke said as she rose to collect forgotten wrapping paper and ribbons, a warning in her tone.

"Oh, my mistake." He grinned. Saint tried to focus on what Olly was showing him on the tablet, but Brooke kept bending over to pick things up. It was very distracting. When she was finally done, he relaxed a little bit until he realized she'd gone down the hall to the bedrooms and been gone for a while.

"What's Mum doing? Did she say?"

"I don't know. Why do you always want to know where she is?"

"I'll explain it when you're older."

"I hate when grown-ups say that," he sneered, his gaze still fixed on the tablet. Saint glanced toward the hallway again, but he couldn't hear her coming.

"Olly."

"What?"

"Look at me for a second."

Hesitantly, the boy dragged his gaze up to Saint.

"What do you think about me dating Mum?"

"Dating her?" The boy scrunched his nose in thought. "Like, kissing and stuff? Did she change her mind? I told you she would."

"Yes, kissing her, but also taking care of her. Making her laugh, buying her presents, cooking for her, watching TV together."

His face cleared. "Oh. That'd be fine."

"You might have to get babysat more often, so Mum and I can go out alone."

"That's okay. Uncle Judson lets me stay up late and eat sweets."

I'm sure he does. "All right. As you were."

As Olly went back to the tablet, Saint saw her standing in the shadowed hallway. She'd gotten dressed into jeans and a green T-shirt that said, "Don't get your tinsel in a tangle." She crooked a finger at him and he rose to meet her.

"How many of these T-shirts do you have?" he muttered, feigning annoyance.

"Never enough."

Saint grunted his disagreement, and she tugged him around the corner.

"So?" she whispered.

"So what?" he whispered back, tucking her hair behind her ear.

"So what did Olly say?" She was biting her thumbnail. "I heard what you asked, but not what he said."

He pulled her hand away from her mouth and kissed her, pressing her lightly against the wall, grinning. "Why, are you nervous?"

"Of course I am!"

Saint chuckled. "He said he hopes it's a shotgun wedding; he requests a brother."

"Low blow, Captain."

"Sorry." He grinned. "He was fine with it. The kid loves me."

"Yes, he does. That's what scares me."

"Brooke," he said, frustrated, "stop worrying for five seconds and just enjoy this moment. It's your favorite day with your favorite people."

"Hmm." She looked up at him. "You're good at enjoying the moment."

"Yes. I excel at it. You have an opportunity to learn from the best. You'd best take notes." Despite her doe-eyed innocence, he could see her vixen side coming out again.

"If today's about favorites, does that mean we get to do my favorite activity too?"

"That depends," he breathed, not daring to hope, but relishing the banter. "What's your favorite activity? And don't you dare say cleaning." She was the sneaky kind of sexy, he'd decided; she hid it under casual clothes, but underneath the disguise, she was more enticing than any woman he'd ever encountered in any club. He had no idea how he was going to keep his hands to himself, now that he had the green light to get closer to her.

"Put your hands on the wall," she instructed, and he complied immediately. "Close your eyes." Even if she hadn't ordered him, they would've fluttered shut on their own when he felt her cool hands slip under his sweatshirt, caressing his chest, smoothing up and down his sides, tracing his ribs. He shivered, and he could feel her smile against his neck as her hands moved to his back.

"This is your favorite activity?" He murmured, angling his head to kiss whatever he could reach.

"Well, it's a tough call, but—" She suddenly pushed away from the wall, and his arms fell around her shoulders. "Thank you for the hug, Captain Saint. I really needed a good hug."

He turned his head to see Olly peering up at them, tablet still in hand. "I'm hungry. Can we eat cinnamon buns now?"

"Sure, kiddo," she chirped, her light tone obviously forced. She froze until Olly disappeared back around the corner, then sighed and slumped against Saint's shoulder, and he laughed.

"Smooth, Everleigh." She pinched his nipples hard in retaliation, and he jumped. "Hey! Easy, I'm just kidding." He wrapped her in a real hug and pressed a soft kiss to her temple. "Let's go eat."

The cinnamon buns had been shaped like a Christmas tree, decorated with green icing and colorful sprinkles for the ornaments. It was adorable, and he greedily packed away two while he watched her try to make bacon and eggs before he took over.

They played both the new games, he wore his scarf, stealing kisses when Olly's attention was elsewhere. He was genuinely surprised when he looked up to see that five hours had passed. He left when her mom arrived, even though they assured him he didn't have to; he needed to make an appearance with his own family, too.

Fuyumi greeted him at the door. "You spent the morning with Brooke and Olly?" she asked in Imaharan.

"Yes."

"And did you enjoy yourself?"

"Very much."

He knew she was trying to bite back a smile, but she failed. "I am glad."

"It's nothing serious yet . . ." Her opinion was more important than he'd let himself admit, and he hated it when he let her down.

"Yes, so you have both said. And yet, I too have eyes."

He gave her a flat smile and switched to Common Tongue. "What's that supposed to mean, Mum?"

She hugged him around his chest, patting his back, continuing in Imaharan. "I know what I see, son. A man looked at me that way once. I married him."

"Dad still looks at you that way."

"What way is that?" she asked. "I thought you didn't know what I was talking about."

"Is there eggnog?" Saint asked, gently guiding her further into the house, and she laughed at him, reaching up to pat his cheek affectionately.

CHAPTER TWENTY-SIX

THE ATMOSPHERE AT BLUFFTON was jovial, celebratory, as they walked in. Dukes, duchesses, ambassadors, governors, and other government employees were mingling, laughing. Champagne was flowing, and everyone was sparkly and polished in their tuxedoes and long evening gowns. Brooke had to admit that Rachel had pulled it off; her cousin had lent her a silver sequined dress with a low back that cinched up her waist, and she *felt* amazing. Saint was in a black tuxedo, and while she loved his normal blue uniform, the tuxedo was making her feel a little . . . swoony. Brooke squeezed Saint's hand, and he squeezed hers back, giving her a tender look.

"You look amazing, did I tell you that?" he asked.

"Twice," she said, smiling coyly.

But the atmosphere shifted immediately when Edward saw her. The glacial look on the king's face told her exactly what he was thinking.

"You didn't ask him if I could come?" she whispered.

"It's fine," Saint said. "You're with me." But he didn't disguise the edge in his voice well enough.

The crowd around Edward suddenly scattered in all directions.

"Game room. Now," Edward bit out, leading the way out of the ballroom back into the hall. They followed him, and she noticed the grand duchess and Saint's friend Sam, who'd taken her to the police station after the break-in, followed as well.

"We discussed this, Captain," Edward said, pacing in front of him.

Saint nodded. "We did. But I'm reopening the discussion, because compared to what I feel for her now, she might as well have meant nothing to me then."

"And yet the risks are the same. I can't have a reporter in the private areas of the palace. I can't have you socializing with someone who could leak sensitive information, the kind of information your job requires you keep secret."

"She knows about Calynda. She's known for months, even before we were close. She could've used it to embarrass me, discredit me. She didn't. She's got so much integrity, I don't know where she keeps it all. So before you walk around all high and mighty, you might take five minutes to actually get to know this person who's extremely important to me before you pass judgment, Edward. I'd think our fifteen-year friendship has at least earned me that much." He turned to Brooke. "We're leaving."

"Wha—" she started.

"I said *we're leaving*. If he's going to treat you like this, we're out of here. We'll find you a glass of champagne somewhere else."

"Now wait just a moment," Edward said sharply, stepping in front of him. Saint shoved him aside, and Brooke heard the grand duchess suck in a shocked breath. The king grabbed Saint's left bicep, and though Saint tried to shake him off, Edward's grip was strong.

"Get the jack out of my way."

"No."

Saint swung at Edward, who deftly ducked out of the way, dropping his hold to lift his hands in front of his chest defensively.

"You gonna fight me, mate?" The two came chest to chest, gazes locked, fists balled at their sides.

"Stop it, both of you! This is insane!" Abbie cried. "Sam, do something!" Their other friend seemed rooted to the spot in shock. The grand duchess, who had a reputation for jumping into the fray, just stood there, with one hand on her belly. Brooke's instincts recognized the gesture. *She's pregnant?* There was no time to think on it, as the king's security came running in, but Edward signaled them to stay back. She felt her own fear rising; would Saint be charged with assault if he hit the king? Or treason? Would he be court-martialed?

Then Saint pushed him, their eyes still locked, and she could see both their self-control eroding quickly. Edward stepped back to regain his balance. *Well, that's my cue, I guess.* Brooke darted between them, throwing her arms around Saint, pinning his arms to his chest.

"You're not going to hit him, babe," she said, her voice low.

"Yes, I am. He's practically begging for it."

"No, he's not. He thinks he's protecting both of you, and you think you're defending me. But I don't need to be defended. I appreciate the thought, but I can fight my own battles. And if your friend doesn't want me here, I'll just leave."

"You shouldn't have to." He squirmed half-heartedly against her hold. "He could take my word for it, for once."

"What exactly are you implying?" Edward stepped forward, but Abbie pulled him back.

"I'm implying I thought you trusted me more than that. I would never bring someone here who would betray you. I can't believe you think I would."

"Isn't it possible that you just don't see the situation for what it is? That you're blinded by lust to her ulterior motives? I know you have the dubious luxury of inviting strangers into your life all the time; I do not. Being in this room makes you family to me; I'm not there yet with her. That's all I was trying to express." Shaking off his wife, Edward turned and marched out of the room. Brooke released Saint just as the grand duchess whirled on him.

"You're an idiot," she snarled. "I was warming him up for you, he was coming around. You know he doesn't like feeling pressured; you know he needs time to think things over. But you had to push the issue and show up here and throw a match on the pile." She hurried out after her husband, leaving Sam, Brooke, and Saint standing in the game room.

"Well . . . ," said Sam. "Well, that went poorly."

"Yeah," Saint replied, running a hand over his face. "You said it, brother."

Sam started back to the main party, and Brooke started doing the relationship math in her head. *If I can't be here, and Saint won't come to social events here without me, then Saint can't be here. If Saint can't be here, it's going to influence his job and his friendship with Edward. If it affects his relationship with Edward, he's going to lose a very important friend and maybe his job.*

Sigh. "You know what has to happen now," Brooke said softly.

"No," he bit out. "I don't accept that, Everleigh. I don't . . ." He stopped when he saw the resignation she knew was written on her face. "Don't do this. Please. Give me more time."

"I'm sorry," she said through tears, pushing up to her toes to press a small kiss to his cheek. "Thank you for trying."

CHAPTER TWENTY-SEVEN

BROOKE HAD JUST DROPPED Olly off at school when her phone rang. It was stupid to send him for one day of the new semester, but there was no one to watch him while she finished packing.

"Hello?" she said, plugging her other ear to hear better over the noise of clattering wagon wheels and parents calling after their children.

"Ms. Brooke Everleigh?" a crisp female voice asked.

"Speaking."

"Please hold for His Majesty, King Edward."

Oh sugar. Sugar sugar sugar.

"Ms. Everleigh. Good morning." She couldn't hang up on the king; that would be a terrible thing to do. But since her mind literally would not function, she felt it might be the safest option. She cringed as she opened her mouth, having not one clue what was going to come out of it.

"Good morning, Your Majesty. How can I help you?" Oh good, her brain had decided to engage. *How nice.* Added bonus: what it produced was not complete garbage.

"I was hoping for the opportunity to speak with you in person this morning. Might you be available to meet?"

"Meet?" she squeaked. "You want to . . . meet?" *Oops, spoke too soon on the "not garbage" ruling. Well, good try, brain.*

"If you're available, yes. Or perhaps there's another time in your schedule that would suit you better? Although I wouldn't quite blame you if you didn't wish to speak with me after last night's unfortunate circumstances."

"Is that what the kids are calling a near fistfight between old friends?" *Hot garbage. That's what that was. My brain just gave me middle-of-summer, noontime garbage, complete with flies.* There was a beat of silence, and then Edward laughed. It wasn't the chuckle she usually saw on the news, if he was being polite. He was *belly-laughing.*

"I wouldn't have the slightest clue what the kids are calling it, but I believe the diplomats would approve my description over yours, and that's with whom I spend most of my time."

A man who knows how to use whom. *Interesting.*

"So will you join me? I promise no punches will be thrown, unless you wish to throw them yourself."

"Of course, Your Majesty. It would be my pleasure." She realized too late that it sounded like she was planning to use her fists on him, and she rolled her eyes at herself.

"What time shall I expect you?"

"I can come now, if that works for you . . . so about an hour?"

"Excellent, Ms. Everleigh. I look forward to our meeting. Let me pass you back to Ms. Scrope for instructions about getting into my residential wing . . ."

"Great." Her hands had stopped shaking by the time she hung up. The train ride to the palace felt anything but normal, knowing she was about to go behind the curtain, knowing she was about to be face-to-face with the man she'd accused of a terrible crime—*falsely* accused. The trembling came back when she was ushered by his private secretary, Ms. Scrope, past the offices she'd seen Saint and the palace staff enter down the hall and on to his residence.

I'm going inside the king's quarters. This is weird. Whose life is this, anyway?

The room was clean, modern, in calming blues and whites. She could see the ocean out the floor-to-ceiling windows. Edward rose and shook her hand as she entered the room, despite the lecture she'd been given about not touching him. His wife stayed seated, sipping from a large mug, in a blue paisley wing-back chair, her legs curled under her in a pinstriped skirt, paired with a cashmere cardigan.

"I've asked my wife, the grand duchess, to join us, since we were both present for the incident last night. She even put on proper clothes for you. You should feel honored, Ms. Everleigh."

"I was already dressed, you punk." There was no malice in her words; she smiled at him warmly. "Don't make it sound like you twisted my arm." She turned to Brooke. "Please call me Abbie."

Brooke nodded mutely, still feeling very surreal. She was misaligned inside, like a boxy, disjointed abstract painting. A staggered, rudimentary combination of her previous portrait, better rooted in reality.

"Tea?" The king paused next to the tray, poised to serve her.

Say something . . .

"What kind?" she asked, sinking into the couch. "Wait, sorry. It doesn't matter. Yes, please." She grimaced. "I'm sorry, I don't . . . I haven't any manners sometimes."

"I like her already," Abbie quipped.

Edward gingerly passed her the hot teacup on a matching saucer. "That reminds me: I've asked you here to offer you an apology." He looked at the carpet, and she saw the deep shame that had engulfed him. "I'm sorry you had to see that last night. Saint and I are indeed old friends, and old friends sometimes carry old wounds. I don't know how much you know about his upbringing, but Saint's had a rough go of it at times. That he's willing to fight with me over you . . . that speaks volumes. I falsely assumed that this was another fling and not something more. I should've listened to him before it came to that."

"He also should've asked before he brought me to your home. Don't let him completely off the hook," Brooke said, letting the blue china teacup warm her fingers.

"Well, I'm sorry for my contribution to the fracas. It was not only unbecoming of a royal, it was a terrible introduction into our circle of friends. That's not how we are with each other, and I hope you can forgive me."

He glanced at Abbie, who gave a nod of agreement.

"And I'm sorry, too," his wife added. "I shouldn't have shouted. Not that I'm ever terribly cultured, but . . . I hope we didn't shock you or scare you."

"No, I was fine. I was mostly concerned that I might come between you." She blushed. "Well, I *did* come between you, but only to protect you. I don't wish to come between you in a negative or unprofitable way. Bros before . . . well, you know."

He chuckled. "Yes, I believe I'm familiar with the expression. And I appreciate the sentiment as well, that you value our friendship over the fledgling romance that appears to be happening between you two. Admittedly, I don't have much experience with choosing a mate . . ." He glanced tenderly at his wife, who grinned at him over her teacup. "But I imagine it's a process fraught with pain and indecision."

"In some ways. And yet, Saint and I . . . we have a strong connection. My own upbringing wasn't perfect, either. We understand each other; if there's enough push and pull in a relationship, you can find yourself dancing in no time rather than falling down."

Edward sat back, his arms clasped over one knee as it rested on the other leg, staring at her. A long moment passed, and Brooke began to sweat under his steady gaze.

"Well, I'm sure you have many pressing matters to attend to—as do I—but thank you for coming in, Ms. Everleigh. I really do appreciate the opportunity to apologize in person."

Her conscience was nudging her at the mention of apologies. "I would also like to apologize, Your Majesty, for accusing you based on Mrs. Burnham's testimony . . . It was obviously ill-advised, and I hope it did no long-term damage."

"Forgiven, I assure you. Your heart was in the right place." That was a relief . . . and yet she was still preoccupied with Saint. He'd been quiet on the way home the night before. Broody. It was making her anxious, knowing she was upsetting him so much.

"Does he know I'm here, sir?" Brooke asked.

"No, not yet. My meeting with him is later today; he needed to prepare for the briefing this morning. Not that he's speaking to me."

Abbie chuckled. "So it should be a short meeting at least." She stood. "If you'll excuse me, I have to get my stuff together for class."

"If I may . . ." Brooke hesitated. It was a chance to show them she was trustworthy. If she was right, they'd know she was on their side. If she was wrong, well, she likely wouldn't see them much anyway. She cleared her throat. "If I may," she said softly, "I'd like to offer my congratulations on your pregnancy."

Abbie paled, and her eyes cut to her husband, who just chuckled.

"Now how in the wide world did you know that? She told me only a week ago."

Brooke smiled a little, even though her heart was heavy. "I'm a mum. And a reporter. She didn't jump into the fight for a reason." She stood up. "We likely won't see each other again, as I'm moving to Gardenia next week. You needn't fear. I won't say anything."

Edward's brow furrowed. "Moving? Saint's said nothing . . ."

Her heavy heart went leaden, sinking to the bottom of her stomach; she'd hoped Saint was dealing with it better emotionally, reaching out for support. "He's in denial. After what happened last night, I think it's for the best."

"I see." He still looked unhappy. "Well, best of luck to you in your future endeavors, Ms. Everleigh," he said, stepping forward to shake her hand again.

"And best of luck to us," said Abbie, "dealing with Saint's surly self once you're gone. You really have brightened his life. The difference has been obvious."

Brooke's lip trembled; she couldn't stand here and listen to how much she'd meant to him. It was too painful. "The feeling is mutual, Your Highness." Brooke Everleigh hurried to the door before she cried in front of her king and his wife.

CHAPTER TWENTY-EIGHT

FLIGHT DELAYED. Perfect. Sure, that made sense. She had literally nowhere else to go. She had a heartbroken, anxious five-year-old with her without anyone to back her up. And now this storm that was coming in meant they'd either have to haul all their suitcases to a hotel or sleep at the airfield. Any one of her friends would let her and Olly crash with them, but Brooke couldn't stomach the idea of saying goodbye to anyone again. The budget would just have to stretch—again.

Brooke watched the snow falling harder now, so thick she couldn't see the individual flakes anymore, just a white blur outside the large windows. She put her e-reader back in her messenger bag. There was no point in just sitting there holding it, and if she put it under the seat, she'd probably forget it. Leaning down, Brooke unzipped her boots and slipped them off in order to tuck her knees into her chest. Olly was lying on his back with his feet up, headphones on, tablet propped up against his knees, taking two seats, but she couldn't bring herself to care.

That's when she saw him across the atrium, his gaze tense and searching, holding a bouquet of red roses that must have set him back a pretty penny this time of year. Her heart lurched forward, as though it wanted to burst through her chest and race to him on its own if her legs wouldn't cooperate.

Are you saying I'll end up with Saint anyway if I leave? she'd asked Judson.

Perhaps. If it's meant to be, he'd answered.

Brooke didn't believe in fate. She'd worked hard to get where she was. And yet . . . And yet it did feel like the universe was trying to tell her something, like the strange holiday magic she'd been feeling so much this season had overflowed into the new year, prompting her to choose a different path than the one she'd set out. The question was whether she'd listen or stubbornly soldier on.

He didn't see her amidst the glut of holiday travelers. She could let him go by, let him move on to search another terminal . . . except she couldn't.

"Saint."

He turned at the sound of her voice, his face lighting up. "I thought I'd missed you."

"You should have." She pointed to the screen overhead. "Flight delayed."

He grinned, and she scowled at him. "More strange magic?"

She squeezed her legs tighter. "I don't know anymore."

"Well," he said, taking a knee in front of her, "I know one thing. That kiss I gave you didn't work at all. You've the worst luck of anyone I ever met."

"I do, don't I?" She laughed, trying to swallow down the hot tears that pressed against her eyes at the joy of seeing his face again. "I had a one-night stand once—one stinking time—and I got pregnant. I mean, what are the odds?"

He shrugged, his gaze never leaving her face.

"I got my dream job, but screwed it up immediately by trusting the wrong people for the right reasons." She tucked her hair behind her ears, feeling vulnerable under his focused attention. "I get robbed and they don't even steal my stupid defective appliances so I could get new ones with the insurance money. Then I fall in love with an amazing guy, but I can't be with him because I got my dream job, then got fired, and now I can't even leave this stupid place." Emotion welled up inside her. She wanted him to hold her, but it wouldn't be fair to ask that of him.

"You're in love with me?" Saint's voice was rough.

Brooke nodded, brushing away a tear. "Not that it matters now."

"It matters. Of course it matters." He put the flowers on the industrial carpet, moving his hands to cover hers, resting on her knees. "I talked to Edward, and he told me that you know about . . ." He glanced around. "That you know what Abbie gave him for Christmas. But you said nothing to Miranda."

She shrugged one shoulder. "It's not my business."

"You could've fixed your career with that information."

She shook her head slowly. "No. That's not me."

"I know it's not." He took her face in his hands. "But now Edward knows that, too. Please stay. He knows he can trust you now." He pressed closer to her.

"I already got a new job," she whispered. "I can't."

"We'll find you another one."

"No one's going to hire me here."

"You've never run from a fight in your life, remember? We can do this. We can figure this out."

"I've nowhere to live, I've already sent my belongings on . . ."

"So have your mum send them back. You can stay with me until we find you a place." He had that look again. That pinched look around his eyes that told her he was searching for words, groping for something to adequately express himself. She held her breath, waiting to see if he'd offer the reassurance that she so desperately needed.

"Please, Brooke. I'm in love with you, too. I want a life with you, you and Olly both. Please don't leave now, just when it's getting so good. It's only going to get better. I know I'm a bastard, I know that. I can't promise anything except that I'm determined not to be that way with you. Will you take a chance on me?"

"I thought you didn't do feelings talk," she whispered, her eyes wide. Her mascara must have been running badly by now.

He rested his forehead against her leg. "I'm learning. I'm trying. It's really jackrabbit hard."

"I see that." She hesitated, then lifted her hand to lightly scratch his scalp, and his shoulders dropped at the contact. *Will you dance with me?* To be real with her, he needed a touch of the person's skin, as if reminding himself that she too was flesh and blood. And that she wasn't retreating just because he said something from his heart. "Thank you for telling me that."

"Just thank you?"

Oh, screw this. Besides the free meals, I would've hated being a restaurant reporter, anyway.

"No, I didn't say that." She felt him tense, holding his breath. "You're the worst, you know that? Couldn't you have told me you loved me while I still had a lease, while I still had internet?"

Saint lifted his head, and his smile was blinding. "I'll call the internet provider. I'll find you a place."

"You'll have to. My luck is still the worst in every way." She smiled at him. "Well, every way except one, perhaps." She leaned toward him for a kiss when a nasal voice came over the loudspeaker.

"Attention, all passengers flying to Gardenia," came a voice over the intercom. "Flight 541 has been cancelled. Please see the agent at the front desk in order to rebook your travel."

As angry passengers rushed the poor gate agent, Brooke took the opportunity to kiss her boyfriend as much as she wanted to, confident that no one would even notice.

CHAPTER TWENTY-NINE

"YOU'VE GOT MY NUMBER?" Brooke asked.

"Yes," Charlie confirmed patiently for the third time. Saint felt the man had been very accommodating through all this, agreeing to what made Brooke happy even when he didn't have to, legally.

"And you're not going anywhere, just hanging out here?" she asked.

"You already asked that, love," Saint put in gently, tugging her toward the door. "Let's go." The three of them had decided it made sense to have Charlie come to Brooke's apartment for their first solo visit. The couple would go for a walk and give the father and son some time together. But Saint had underestimated Brooke's freak-out when she actually had to leave her baby alone with his dad.

"We'll be back in a little while, all right?" Brooke said over her shoulder to Olly, who looked a little uncertain about this whole idea. *That's not helping.* Saint gave the man a glare that communicated all the resources at his disposal to hurt the man if the kid got so much as a paper cut, then he dragged a teary Brooke out of her apartment.

"I can't do this."

"Yes, you can. He seems like a nice guy. It'll be fine."

"No, it won't." She was breathing hard, and he hoped she wouldn't have a panic attack. Saint rubbed her back through her winter coat. "You thought he was nice enough when he impregnated you . . ."

"That's different. And I was young. What did I know? Nothing."

"Come on, love. Trust me. He's his dad. He's a little green, but he's been good with him so far. You wanted Olly to get to know him, remember?"

"I don't think I ever said that," she grumped, starting to calm down, wiping her nose on the back of her mitten. He chatted with her about other things as they walked to the train, trying to take her mind off Olly and Charlie. It was entirely selfish; he had his own problems he was trying not to think about. And they were almost there, to the prison gates.

He'd called Calynda a few times, responded when she initiated contact, but he was still nervous as Jersey. This confrontation had been building for so long . . . With all the practice he was now getting expressing his feelings, though, it just seemed like it was time to try it with her, too. It could hardly make things worse.

Saint couldn't let go of Brooke's hand. He knew he should give Calynda a hug; she'd been in jail, for Woz's sake. But he needed contact with Brooke as much as his next breath, which was condensing in front of him. He watched as Calynda walked toward them—no purse, no coat, just a paper bag.

"They stole my stuff again," she said. "Dirty cops." Noticing their joined hands, she slowed her steps and lifted an eyebrow. "Who's this, baby?"

"Calynda, this is my girlfriend, Brooke."

"You don't have girlfriends."

"Except this one." He cleared his throat. "We need to talk, Calynda. You can't keep doing this to me. It feels shitty. It feels .

. ." His words stalled, and Brooke gave his hand a quick squeeze. "It makes me feel used."

Calynda's eyes filled with tears. Saint didn't know if it was real emotion or if she was manipulating him, but it didn't really matter. He knew what he needed to do.

"So I'm willing to take you to a rehab clinic. But I'm not letting you back into my life until you're clean." He cleared his throat again. *Why is this so hard?* "Brooke and I are getting married soon. If you're clean, you can come to the wedding and sit with the Makis." He wasn't going to put Oliver in the middle of this dumpster fire of a relationship; she could find out about him later. He wouldn't make the boy a pawn in their stupid game.

"You got a smoke?" she asked, and he shook his head slowly. "You don't have to worry about me, baby. I went through detox the hard way on the inside."

"Yes, but you didn't attend classes or counseling about addiction." He took a step closer to her. "You need those. You need to really work on this, Mum, not just dry out in jail, and then run right out when things get hard and take it up again. You need emotional tools."

She snorted, her eyes wary. "What do you know about it?"

"Nothing. Except that I'm the same way. Chasing a different kind of high, but it's there." He looked at Brooke, keeping his eyes on her face, even though he was still talking to Calynda. "And I've needed to grow through it, grow into a new set of skin. It's tougher, even though it's more tender."

Brooke was gazing back at him, and he felt all her support, her strength, seeping into him. It made sense, since his head, hands, and neck were literally wrapped in her knitted love.

Calynda shook her head, digging around in her pockets and pulling out a package of cigarettes she'd apparently had all along. "You think you know so much," she said quietly, her tone more bitter than the biting cold that was painting his cheeks red.

"All I know is I've got a lot to learn. You've got my number if you change your mind, but I'm not giving you any money but for counseling. So don't ask. I care about you. I'm not doing you any favors by enabling your addiction." He turned and pulled Brooke behind him as he strode away from the jail.

"You're a poor excuse for a son!" she shouted after him. "How dare you judge me? I knew you'd walk out on me, just like your rotten father! You're a bad apple after all."

The trembling started in his hands, but the cold and Brooke's firm grasp covered it, made it more bearable.

"I'm proud of you," she whispered, and he squeezed her hand. "I'm so proud, I'm bursting. I'm going to kiss away all those nasty things she said."

"I'll let you."

Around the corner now, she pulled him to a stop. "Seriously. That's rubbish. Utter rubbish. You're a good apple. The best apple I know. My favorite apple, the apple I love."

"Stop saying 'apple,'" he teased as he leaned forward to kiss her. He used as much tongue as he felt he could get away with in public, and he wasn't sorry when he was rewarded with the needy look in her eyes when he pulled away. "Thank you for coming with me."

"Thank you for letting me. It was a welcome distraction."

He squeezed her around her shoulders as he turned them back toward the sidewalk.

"Saint?"

"Hmm?"

"We're getting married soon?"

Oh shiitake. I said that, didn't I? He kicked himself internally. He'd been planning to ask her properly; he'd been thinking so much about the right way to do it, dwelling so often on the hard feelings he'd have to say out loud, he forgot that her yes wasn't a foregone conclusion. Apparently, his embarrassed silence spoke loud enough, because Brooke chuckled.

"Have you picked a venue? A date?"

"Of course not. I thought you might like to be involved in the planning."

"But not in the decision?"

"I was getting to that, I just . . . Don't make me talk about this now, all right? I've got things planned, you're not going to wring a hasty proposal out of me."

She laughed again. "No, you're right. What was I thinking?"

He was so close to knowing; they had some relative privacy for once, and it would make the lead-up a lot easier, already knowing what she'd say. "Will you, though?" he asked, not stopping, not daring to look at her.

"Yes," she said, squeezing his hand, and when he turned toward her, Brooke's smile warmed him down to his toes. He kissed her quickly, unable to help himself.

"Let's go get Ol. Surely Charlie's sugared him up enough by now."

CHAPTER THIRTY

"I HAVE COPIES OF MY recommendations and résumés, my breath is fresh, my heels are high, I'm wearing my power bra, I have Judson's lucky pen. What am I forgetting?"

Saint's eyebrows jumped. "Power bra?"

Brooke rolled her shoulders and her neck. "Yes. This bra makes me feel like a badass. My girls look amazing in it. Every woman should have one."

He kept a straight face. "Is it a certain brand, or . . ."

Brooke grinned at him. "One is enough, thanks."

"Just curious," he said, holding his hands up in faux innocence. "I know what you're missing: a kiss for luck." He moved in, but she shoved him back onto his heels.

"That didn't work last time, and you'll screw up my make-up."

Undeterred, he reclaimed the space. "Good, they'll know you're taken."

She put a hand on his chest. "I can communicate that myself if it comes up." She looked toward the building, but could still see he was pouting, that sweet lower lip poking out, in her peripheral vision. "Honestly, you're a worse sport than Olly when you don't get your way." She held up a finger. "One kiss."

His wolfish grin conveyed his excitement over the minor victory.

"No, no. I mean it, Captain. One small peck. Do not screw up my look. I mean it."

"Yes, ma'am." He came in slow, shuffling his whole body forward, sliding one hand behind her neck, caressing her cheek with the knuckles of the other.

"Just do it already," she grumped, her nerves getting the better of her.

"But if I only get one, I want to make sure it's a good one." He looked down at her with incredible warmth, his blue eyes sparkling. "Who am I kidding?" he murmured, "you're gonna knock 'em dead in there. This is more for me, really." His lips were so close to hers, she could feel his minty breath tickling her face. Even that small bit of him made her heart race.

"You're killing me, Captain."

"That's the idea. With every kiss I give you, I'm trying to steal your heart."

"You can't steal something that's already yours," she whispered, squeezing his hand, "so I think you can relax. You're worth sticking around for, trust me."

"Relaxing is new for me," he whispered back. "I'm not used to it . . ." He finally closed the distance between them, and the sheer sweetness of the kiss nearly knocked Brooke off her very high heels. "But I'm getting there. Now get in there, tiger, I don't want to make you late."

She pointed at him, and he pointed back.

She followed the receptionist back to the conference room, where five other women were waiting. The editor rose and gave her a firm handshake, introducing Brooke to the other department heads as she closed the door.

"I must say, Ms. Everleigh, it's not every day that we get a letter of reference from the king, especially considering your history with the royal family."

Brooke fought a blush. "Obviously, I was very wrong to accuse him without enough proof . . ."

She held up a quelling hand. "But I admire your courage. Your willingness to jump into the issue, tackle it head-on. That's one thing we're looking for in our reporters. Your writing is crisp, your perspectives are fresh, and you've obviously got tenacity."

They asked questions—a lot of questions. But they seemed to be working out where she might fit best in the company rather than deciding whether to offer her a job. That suspicion was confirmed when they asked her to step out so that they could briefly confer.

"We'd like to offer you a position in features. It'll give you a chance to profile prominent women, people with something to say. A better fit than politics, perhaps."

"That's great," she breathed, feeling like her chest didn't have a brick on it for the first time in weeks. "Thank you, I'm thrilled to be working with you. Thank you so much for the opportunity, you won't regret bringing me on."

"I'm sure we won't." The editor smiled. "So now that the interview is officially over . . ." The woman leaned closer, lowering her volume. "Who was that we saw you with outside?"

She was going to kill Saint. It would be a slow, painful death involving several kitchen implements. "That's my fiancé."

"Does he have a brother?"

"Technically, yes, but if you're hoping for the same make and model, they're out of stock." She glanced at him through the window, and he waved, that crooked smile melting her heart again. "He's one of a kind." All the women waved back, then sighed.

"You're so lucky."

Brooke chuckled. "Yes, I am."

EPILOGUE

THE RECESSIONAL FADED as the doors swung shut behind Saint and Brooke. She'd dragged him into the green room where she'd gotten ready for the wedding, hoping for a brief moment of privacy before they had to go on to the reception. He collapsed onto the fuzzy brown couch, still tired from the bachelor's party two nights ago.

"Still think it was a waste of time to learn my name?"

He grinned and pulled her down onto his lap. "You'll regret that sass when you're finally panting *my* name in a few hours."

She tenderly laced her fingers into his hair, and he grabbed her wrists before she could destroy his styling. "But what name shall I use?" she teased, wriggling on his lap. "Surely not 'Captain' . . ."

"I've been called worse."

"Saint?"

"That'd be fine."

"Francis?"

He paused. "Say it again."

Brooke stared into his eyes, her china blue depths warming. "Francis." Then, confirming herself as the sneaky vixen he already knew she was, his wife leaned forward and put her ruby-red lips right next to his ear and said it again on a tortured sigh. "Francis." His blood heated to boiling instantly. He felt his control lift away from him like a kite caught on a sudden gust of wind, the string whipping through his fingers; he was sure to get rope burn if he tried to stop things now. Brooke squealed as he stood up and carried her to the closet . . . then realized both his hands were on her legs, supporting her. If he put her down, she'd run off for sure.

"Open the door, Everleigh."

"It's Saint, if you don't mind, and I will not. You'll bed me properly our first time, not in a rush next to the disinfectant. I have waited a long time for this. Much longer than you."

He growled as he pressed her back against the closet door and pinned her there, crashing his mouth into hers. "Woman, I've had your taste in my mouth since you drunkenly attacked me that night. I've been good. I've waited. But now you're mine; open the jacking door, Mrs. Saint."

"Just a little longer," she murmured, caressing his jawline. "What's your record?"

He adjusted his hold to lift her higher. "Record?"

She nodded, dropping a languid kiss to his lips. "Number of times in one night."

He had to think. Thinking was not so easy with her legs wrapped around him like that. "Four."

"Oh, we can break that easily," she said, giggling.

"I agree; let's start now. Open the door." He jiggled her legs insistently.

"We've got 150 people waiting for us to cut the cake, love, and I can't wrinkle this dress any more."

"You may remove the dress. I'll wait."

"Not happening."

He glared at her, and she glared right back. Her resolve was not weakening. "You have a frustratingly indomitable will, woman."

She pushed him back a little to see his whole face. "I do when it matters," she said. "Remember when I told you I wasn't promising anything? Well, I've changed my mind. In fact, I'm promising everything. You're getting all the care and attention I have to give, sexual or otherwise, my whole heart, whether you want it or not. And my whole heart cannot be communicated in this closet. Because I love you, you donkey." When she sealed her words with a kiss, Saint's heart cracked open and glowed like a road flare.

This is what I get for marrying a writer . . .

"Damn it," he complained, "I hate it when you make more sense than I do." He gently lowered her to the ground and helped her re-fluff her dress, which was in fact already quite wrinkled. He strode to the door, then stopped at the sound of her voice.

"We're breaking that record if it takes all night, Mr. Saint."

He pointed at her, and she pointed back. She turned to the mirror to fix her makeup, and he lingered, watching her. Despite the fact that he hadn't gotten into the closet with her, he somehow felt even luckier than if he had.

Thank you for reading my book!

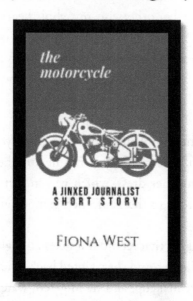

Saint bought himself a very special Christmas present (who deserves it more? He's been a very good boy this year), and the only person he wants to share it with is Brooke. Brooke, however, has other ideas. You can grab this free bonus story *The Motorcycle* when you sign up for my monthly newsletter, The West Wind. Find a screen and follow this link now:
BookHip.com/LTABMZ

MORE BOOKS FROM FIONA WEST

#

The Borderline Chronicles

The Ex-Princess, Abbie and Edward (Book 1)
The Un-Queen, Abbie and Edward (Book 2)
The Almost-Widow, Sam and Tezza (Book 2.5)
The Semi-Royal, Rhodie and Arron (Book 4), coming February 2020, e-book available to pre-order now

Please leave a review!

Whether you loved it or thought it was a dud,
Please leave a review and inform all your buds.
Was Saint extra swoony? Did Brooke make you laugh?
Don't write a novel, just a short paragraph.
Give it some stars that you think fit just right,
And new readers will find it a welcome sight!

Yeah, I'm a novelist, not a poet...but seriously, like all small businesses, reviews and social proof help introduce new readers to my work, which means I can keep writing more books. A review of any length on your favorite platform would be much appreciated.

ACKNOWLEDGEMENTS

- With gratitude to my sweet family, who challenges me and loves me even when I'm being a jerk. Even when I'm a bigger jerk than my main characters.
- Thanks to Rhonda Merwarth, my editor. Your insights were helpful and kind, and that's a rare combination.
- Thanks to Steven Novak, my awesome cover artist. Thank you for being so patient with my indecision.
- Thanks to my writing group, Ruth and Magalie. Your conversations and insights keep my creative juices flowing! (Is that weird? That's probably weird.)
- Thanks to my critique partners, Angela Boord and Rebecca Hopkins, and my beta readers, Christine, Liz and Erin. Your help is invaluable! I wish I had some way to repay your kindness...other than free books, of course.
- Thanks to my sensitivity reader, Sachiko Burton with Salt and Sage Books. Thanks for helping me see the work from another perspective!

Connect with Fiona!

Thanks so much for taking the time to read my work. I hope you enjoyed reading it even more than I enjoyed writing it, though I doubt that's possible. Being an author is a dream come true, and getting to share my books with delightful, thoughtful readers like you just adds to the sweetness. Drop me a line and let me know what you thought or leave a review on Amazon or Goodreads!

Sign up for my monthly newsletter, The West Wind, for freebies, deleted scenes, book reviews, and insight into my writing process.

On Twitter as @FionaWestAuthor

On Facebook as @authorfionawest

On Instagram as @fionawestauthor

On Goodreads as Fiona West

Or email me at fiona@fionawest.net. I love talking to fans!

9 781732 877